MARGARET MAHY

Margaret Mahy was born in New Zealand and has loved telling stories all her life. She has published well over a hundred titles and won several major prizes and awards, including The Order of New Zealand, for her internationally acclaimed contribution to children's literature. She has twice won the prestigious Carnegie Medal (*The Haunting*, 1982, and *The Changeover*, 1984). Margaret lives in the South Island of New Zealand, in a house which she partially built herself, overlooking Governors Bay.

Also by Margaret Mahy

Twenty-four Hours
The Tricksters
Memory

For younger readers

The Riddle of the Frozen Phantom

The Catalogue of the Universe

MARGARET MAHY

Collins flamingo

An imprint of HarperCollinsPublishers

To Penny... Drive Carefully!

First published by J.M. Dent & Sons in 1985
First published in Great Britain by CollinsFlamingo in 2002
CollinsFlamingo is an imprint of HarperCollins*Publishers* Ltd
77-85 Fulham Palace Road, Hammersmith,
London W6 8JB

The HarperCollins website address is:
www.**fire**and**water**.com

1 3 5 7 9 8 6 4 2

ISBN 000 712338 8

Margaret Mahy asserts the moral right to be
identified as the author of this work.

Printed in Great Britain by
Clays Ltd, St Ives plc

Conditions of Sale

CONTENTS

1   Moonshine   7

2   Threats of Invasion   21

3   Family Matters   31

4   The Wobble in the Cemetery of the World   52

5   Encounters in a Changing Street   62

6   On Being a Child of Love   71

7   A Road of Blood and Flowers   84

8   Events are the Stuff of the World   99

9   Foreign Relations   104

10 Mrs Potter Rolls a Cigarette   124

11 Midnight Appointments   141

12 A Step Up in the World   151

13 A Leap into the Abyss   167

14 The Dragon's Cave   179

15 Three-minute Hero   186

16 The Catalogue of the Universe   207

1

MOONSHINE

One hot summer night Angela woke up and found she could not go back to sleep again for, beyond her closed lids, the room was infected with disturbing silver. In the end she gave in to wakefulness in her own stubborn way, getting up but refusing to open her eyes, feeling her way from place to place, choosing to see by touch and memory rather than by an alien light. She was irritated with the moon for invading her sleeping time with a light that was not even its own, but stolen from the sun and hastily passed on, and for looking in at her window with its implacable white face. Her friend Tycho Potter, given as he was to passing on information that not many people particularly wanted to hear, had once told her that an ancient Greek, an Ionian scientist called Anaximander, had been the first person to work out that the moon might shine by reflected light alone.

"Big deal!" Angela had said, but now she remembered Anaximander in spite of herself, for understanding moonlight was not just simple, but another mysterious victory for the human mind.

Angela, eyes tight, groped her way along the settee under

her window, pausing for a moment to feel the glass eyes, bald ears and unravelling nose of her old teddy, and to recall with troubled tenderness its strange, pointed face – more the face of a fox than a bear. Next she found on the windowsill the springtime goldfinch's nest and, beside it, her collection of smooth stones which she held one by one against her lips, cool kisses in the hot, shiny night. Her fingers touched the bowl of potpourri she and her mother, Dido, had made together, sifted the dried, papery petals, and then at last traced the blunt face of the ominous doll, Rebecca, who looked at the world out of narrow, painted eyes that had no human whites to them – a doll-like creature from another planet, inspiring excitement rather than affection. But Angela loved thrilling things just as much as she did kind ones. Then she paused, a fold of Rebecca's skirt pinched between her finger and thumb, and listened. She thought she had heard something – a sound like a whispered word. However, if so, it had been spoken and had gone. There was nothing out in the night but silence and silver. She began her slow exploration again, and came to her desk loaded with notes that would never be read again, hours of work for recent exams, all waiting to be burnt.

Angela, her boyfriend Robin, Tycho Potter and other people from their class were really killing time until the end of the school term released them. School exams were over and useful activities were being organised for them. But it was an odd, artificial time of year. There in the moony night Angela felt no nostalgia for school, though she knew that at eighteen, a big, important part of her life was ending for ever. She was looking forward to the following year when she would be doing a commercial course at the polytechnic, learning not only about typewriters but about word-processors and computers too, entering the science-fiction world of stored memory and working memory, of machine memories at once more precise and more limited than her own (which rebelliously chose what it would remember and what it would forget, according to rules of its own). For many years, for example, she had believed she could remember her father, but Dido said such memory was impossible for her father had never seen her, even when she was a baby. All she really knew was what she had been told, and somehow or other she had turned the stories into a sort of memory of someone red-headed as she was, a taller, broader version of herself in men's clothes. Only recently, however, she had discovered that appearances were not quite so simple.

Suddenly Angela grew tired of her game of blindness, opened her eyes and looked down at herself, quite naked in the moonlight, for she refused to wear a nightgown in summer. Her feet swam, long and pale, in the shadows that seemed to collect around the floor, drawn down by the secret gravity of a house at night, and once again she thought she heard a whispered word, come and gone before it could be truly understood.

Life was full of disadvantages for Angela. Apart from having no accountable father, she lived in a home with an outside lavatory, and drove in a car that rattled and backfired, always threatening to fall to pieces and spill empty apple-juice cans and paperback books with curling covers. But at least she could be confident about beauty. Angela had been given a wonderful dowry by her unknown father. She was her own currency and, being desirable, was able to pay her own way in the ferocious world beyond the fox-faced teddy and the smooth stones. There in her room, with moonshine stripping the fire from her hair and the gold from her skin, she had a moment of feeling grateful for something she generally took for granted.

As she stood, simply feeling grateful, she heard for the third time, beyond all doubt, a sound outside, a sound so soft that it would have been possible to think it out of existence again, except that this time she really *knew* she had heard it, a sound as gentle as a hand brushing down a velvet curtain. It made her curious but it did not alarm her, for she was used to many different sounds in the night, living as she did up above the city, in a wild place close under the sky. She went to her window and looked out, and there in the bright moonlight she saw her mother Dido in the centre of the square of grass half-contained in the right angle made by their odd home (a home that had never quite got as far as being a proper house). It took a moment to realise what Dido was doing, but that rhythmic and dreamy sway was familiar – Dido was scything the grass by moonlight. Angela could see the entranced, semicircular swing of her shoulders, heard the whisper of the keen steel and the sigh of long grass bowing down before her. Everything around her was drenched in a light so clear and so intense it seemed as if it must have more substance than ordinary light. It was the very light of visions and prophecies.

Resting on the shank of her scythe, Dido turned her head and looked straight over at Angela, but the slumberous lid of the verandah was half-closed over the small eye of Angela's bedroom, and besides, Angela could plainly see that Dido's own eyes were so flooded with moonlight that she was radiantly blind, a fairy-tale woman who, having lost her own sight, had been given pale, shining eyes of silver. She looked up into the air, smiled (Angela could see the gleam of her teeth) and returned to her scything.

Angela and Dido lived in a house which Dido was slowly buying, at the top of Dry Creek Road, a road rooted down in the city, but climbing up over the hills, increasingly jostled by wild flowers, weeds, long grasses and golden broom, until all houses stopped. The blue-black asphalt ended with them, and Dry Creek Road became more of a track, in spite of its proud name. As it climbed, it began to swoop and curve, writhing like a desperate serpent pinned down and anxious to be free. A sturdy bridge crossed the great, branching scar of the dry creek from which the road took its name – a creek of barren stones, capable of bearing, after a night of rain, a swollen torrent that would roar like a beast on a continual, angry note as if the hillside itself had found a throat and was issuing a warning. Up above the bridge the road grew leaner and more treacherous, held at bay on one side by a bank alive with moss and ferns and broom and foxgloves, while on the other it surrendered to the void, a great airy fall on to stony slopes far below. Not only this, the road claimed victims just as if it were a serpent god. Hedgehogs, possums, magpies and rabbits were killed by cars, particularly close to the city, for nobody lived near the top except Dido and Angela May, and a morose farmer with the cheerful name of Charlie Cherry. He had two sons, Phil and Jerry Cherry, who often drove by Angela and Dido on the way home, burning past them even on corners, blasting the horn at them, contemptuous of their slow and careful descent.

Watching Dido scythe in the moonlight like Mother Time herself, Angela found herself thinking of the road, and wondering at the same time if Dido might not be just a little crazy. Like the road, Dido had a dangerous edge and sometimes she went right out to it and danced, apparently challenging it to crumble away under her. Angela feared for such a reckless dancer, though by now she knew that she too had an inside road as well as an outside one, and dangerous edges of her own. Still, sooner or later, she confidently expected to find wonderful happiness in life. But whatever Dido challenged by dancing on dangerous edges was no sort of happiness Angela could recognise. Dido scythed on, leaving a swathe of shadow behind her and, half-bent at the window, Angela watched her, pulling on her dressing-gown as she did so.

Over the tops of the trees the sky was deep, deep blue, dark and transparent at the same time, and between the sky and the black frill of the tree tops, the outer edge of the city twinkled, every bit as far away as the stars. In the city somewhere among those lights slept Angela's boyfriend, Robin. The moonlight, if it managed to get into his room, would shine upon his cups and trophies, for he was a notable sportsman – good in so many fields – the best all-rounder in the school. In the city, but hidden from Angela by the trees, Tycho Potter also slept, probably dreaming of stars, or of being good-looking, or perhaps of Angela herself – all unattainable things. Over his bed he had pinned various sayings that had caught his attention. *Chance favours the prepared mind!* was one that Angela remembered. She believed it was true, and tried to keep herself prepared for whatever chance might offer. And perhaps Tycho hoped that, by pinning such thoughts up and sleeping under them and seeing them first thing when he woke up in the morning, he might turn into a sort of latter-day Ionian philosopher himself, able to command the world by observing and predicting.

Dido paused in her scything and turned to inspect her progress.

Now! thought Angela, and leaned out of the window. "Are you OK?" she called, and Dido, not too surprised to be spoken to in the early hours of the morning, answered by asking a question.

"Heavens – what are you doing awake at this time of night?"

"Why are *you* awake, you old, mad mother?" Angela asked, buttoning her dressing-gown. "Same reason as me, I suppose. The old devil moon dipping its finger into our sleep – having a little taste of us!"

"Tasting our dreams, sweet and sour!" Dido said, watching Angela scramble through the window on to the verandah. "But I think it's more like being baptised – total immersion in cold fire, and then we're changed – never the same again."

Angela ignored the old cane chair on the verandah, and chose to sit on the steps, drawing up her long legs and putting her arms around her knees.

"I can't think of one other kid I know who'd wake up at two a.m. and find her mother scything the grass," she said.

"I couldn't sleep, and it needed doing," Dido said. "I didn't mean to do so much, but I got started and began enjoying it, and with all that light around it seemed as if I should use it up in some way."

She came and sat down on the steps too.

"You could have cut your foot off," Angela said severely.

Dido stuck out her feet. Under her dressing-gown she was wearing gumboots.

"I was very careful," she said apologetically, "and I feel I know every bump of the ground. I've gone over it so often. And, once you get going, scything sort of takes over." As she spoke, she took the long steel from her dressing-gown pocket and began sharpening the scythe. "I used to struggle to begin with, but now I'm so used to it I'm sure I enjoy it more than other people enjoy their lawn mowers. It's so silent."

Angela looked around. She thought of her vanished father, and thought that she was surrounded by the light of revelation and prophecy.

"Mum!" she began all in a rush. "Remember you used to tell me about my father when I was a little girl, just as if it was a fairy story."

"It was," said Dido, nodding. "It really was." Angela, listening carefully, tried to work out if her mother's voice had always been so dry and cautious, or if these were expressions that had only crept in over recent weeks.

"You never tell me now," she said, hurt by the caution.

"You know it all by heart," Dido replied, giving her a sideways glance, gentle enough, but also, Angela thought, warning her not to ask any more. It was so hard to be sure when you were seeing by moonshine. "It's so long ago – it's a fossilised dinosaur egg – it'll never hatch. Why have you started pestering me about it all of a sudden?"

"You said you'd love him for ever," Angela cried reproachfully, ignoring the question.

"Yes, but I didn't know then how long for ever was going to be," said Dido.

Angela felt hurt on behalf of her lost father. He was betrayed, and she was being betrayed with him.

"But you did love each other madly," she prompted, determined to make Dido tell the old story once again, sitting on the step in the moonlight. Though she used an ironic voice to make fun of the soap-opera words, she also wanted Dido to admit that they were true.

"OK – yes – we loved each other madly," Dido agreed like a genial parrot.

"But he was married!" Angela declared dramatically, putting her hand on her heart. "It was useless. He owed it to his family to stay and look after them."

"That's right!" Dido said, smiling gently and delicately rubbing the steel along the blade of the scythe.

"But you couldn't bear to let it end like that, so you had *me*," Angela finished impatiently. "Go on, say it! Let me feel chosen again, just like I did when I was little."

"You were chosen," said Dido, laughing. "Come on! You know you're the marvellous person of my life."

This was part of what Angela wanted to be told. She sighed and leaned sideways against Dido. The next part was the tricky bit.

"Supposing you got a chance to see him again..." she began.

"Oh no!" Dido said quickly, not letting her finish her sentence. "I've changed too much, and I'm sure he has too. Besides I'm too tired."

"Still – true love and all that..." Angela said vaguely. "Tycho and I are making a list of romantic ideas, mostly from books..."

"Is that why you were reading *The Sheik* last week?" Dido asked, sounding amused. "Where on earth did you find it?"

"I found it – in a junk shop," Angela said enthusiastically. "We're never likely to get a chance to see the movie. It says, 'He had the handsomest and cruellest face she had ever seen,' and 'she felt the boyish clothes were stripped from her limbs, and her beautiful white body was laid bare.'"

"Get away!" Dido exclaimed, and began sharpening her scythe again.

"And *then* she asked, 'Why have you brought me here?'" Angela recalled, "and *he* said, 'Bon dieu! Are you not woman enough to know?'"

"They don't write lines like that any more," Dido said. "Though probably they do, but somehow I don't get to read them."

"They make me laugh in a way," Angela said, "and yet..." She stared out at the soft night. "It's a bit like *Gone With the Wind* and Rhett Butler carrying Scarlett O'Hara up the grand staircase. It bugs poor Tyke, him being so short. He does weight-lifting and exercises, so he says he could probably get Scarlett O'Hara up off the ground if he had to, but then her feet would keep banging on the stairs. Anyhow *you* count as a romantic notion to us because you sacrificed all for love."

"I didn't sacrifice all – well, I had to put off going to university for eighteen years," Dido said, for she was finishing a degree very slowly, in time left over from working in the office of a film and video hire shop, and from the cooking and conversations of family life. "I don't call that sacrificing all. I took on much more than I gave up. And I'd be an absolute dead loss as a romantic notion these days."

"Suppose I was to try and bring you together again?" Angela asked in a sentimental voice. "With my father, I mean. Little children can do that, when their parents have grown apart. That's a well-known romantic notion."

"Oh, go to bed!" commanded Dido. "I wouldn't know what to say to your father by now. We'd have one of those painful, polite conversations, asking one another what we were going to do over Christmas."

"You could talk about me – your wonderful child!" Angela said, suddenly reaching up as if she would embrace the moon. "Gosh, Tycho's parents talk about his sister all the time. Can you believe it, her name's Africa! It's Africa this and Africa that. It's just as if they've got one real child, and Tyke and Richard are only near misses. Ring him up. Go on! I'd like to meet him."

"Never!" said Dido firmly. She half-turned in order to look directly at Angela. "Listen, Angela. I do love you, and next to you, solitude. That's a fact. There's you, me and silence, and I don't want anything else."

Angela thumped the step irritably.

"How can you want so little?" she asked.

"I've listened to too much noise over the years," Dido said. "Sometimes it's drowned out a lot of other things I should have been listening to. I'm really lucky because I like my own company. What's wrong with that?"

Angela looked up through the layers of pearly air.

"So you won't ring my father or – or get in touch with him in any way and give me a chance to meet him. He's paid for me all these years. He might want to meet me."

"Even if he did, he's too fond of his first family to run any risks," Dido said.

Angela leaned back against the step above, which made an uncomfortable ridge halfway down her back. Suddenly she liked the thought of her own bed and solitude.

"OK – you know best," she said, but found Dido looking at her very narrowly for a moment, before they hugged each other goodnight.

A little later, Angela, in her bed, watched a wand of moonlight move through the bedroom air, touch her breast and turn it from fabulous gold to cool silver. As she lay there, she thought of men. She thought of Robin and the band they were going to hear the following night, and she thought of Tycho, who was not a boyfriend but a different sort of friend, more precious than a boyfriend because he could never be replaced, a possession awkward but rare. She was prepared to put up with many spiky moments with Tycho because every so often he became an enchanter, often without meaning to, or realising what he had done.

Her last thoughts were of her father, who was also sleeping somewhere out there in the moonlit city. Angela knew just where. She had not told Dido, but she knew him by sight, and knew his two addresses, the one of his business in town and the other his home. From the public footpath where anyone was allowed to stand and stare, she had stared up over the big green lawns, seen the pillared front door of his house, noted the swimming pool, the bricked-in barbecue area, the well-kept tennis court of his very expensive house.

On this night of moonshine she went to sleep, half-dreaming of that swimming pool and of the moon that might be reflected in it at this very moment, the same moon Anaximander had guessed about, the same moon she had often seen set squarely in the object lens of Tycho's telescope, the same moon that had filled Dido's eyes with so much silver that moonshine flowed back out of her, lighting up 1000 Dry Creek Road planted high on a hilltop, a house linked to the rest of the world by a snaky road.

2

THREATS OF INVASION

It seemed like the middle of the night when the phone rang, but it was early morning. Tycho Potter woke out of a dream of huge wheels, one turning inside the other. His brother Richard, behind a door on the opposite side of the hall, enjoying the privacy of a room very little larger than a walk-in pantry, leaped up with the confused idea that beetles were walking over his face, but it was merely the unfamiliar tickle of an immature beard against a freshly laundered pillowcase. The curtains were closed, but every window in the house had a thin, bright edge as if framed in silver wire.

The phone spoke again, and a moment later their mother answered it in a voice clouded equally with sleep and apprehension.

"Darling – are you all right?" they heard her say. Both young men in their different rooms muttered, "Africa!" in tones of despair, and pulled the covers over their heads. However, it was a symbolic retreat, not a real one. They were both curious to know what was going on and listened anxiously through their quilts to hear all that there was to be heard. The first thing they heard was their father knocking over the clock that stood on his bedside table in his hurry to get up and get out into the hall, close to the phone.

"Damn!" they heard him mutter, and then he called in a strange, shouting whisper. "What is it? Is she all right?"

But then, feeling he had made a gesture of concern, he lost all interest in possible sleepers and stopped whispering. "That damned husband of hers!" he cried, his voice a curious mixture of distress and triumph.

"Oh dear," Mrs Potter was saying sympathetically as her husband charged into the hall. "Oh, how dreadful. No, of course you don't have to put up with anything like that. Now would you like us to come and get you?"

This was too much for Richard. Tycho heard the thud as he leapt out of bed, followed by the bang of the handle of his bedroom door against the wood panelling in the hall.

"She's married!" Richard began shouting. "Remember? Married! She's got a baby and a husband!"

"She's in trouble of some sort," Mr Potter protested loudly.

"She's always in trouble," Richard shouted back. "That's why she had to get married, remember!"

"No, of course we don't mind," Mrs Potter was saying, and Tycho could tell from her voice that she had shut her eyes, as if not seeing was also a way of not hearing the noisy argument beginning around her.

"That's cheap, Richard, very cheap!" Mr Potter cried reprovingly.

"It's true, Daddy, very true!" Richard replied.

"I'm getting the car out," Mr Potter said in a resigned but determined voice. Africa was his favourite child, he did not like her husband and, although he did not exactly want them to be unhappy, he was not averse to rescuing her from a few troubles from time to time.

"You're mad!" shouted Richard. "Tell her to – tell her to get back into bed and start cleaving to her lawful husband. She was always trying to do that before they were married, and now she's promised to do it until death does them part."

"That's all right, dear! No! Nothing to worry about," Mrs Potter was saying. Tycho raised himself on one elbow, and then, sighing, scrambled out of bed himself.

"She promised it in a church!" Richard went on implacably. "I'll never forget the trouble you had finding one that would take the responsibility for blessing her. And if she comes home she'll have to bring her baby too – think about that!"

Mrs Potter must have heard this, closed eyes and all, for as Tycho wandered out into the hall he heard his mother saying rather desperately, "Oh, wait a moment, dear – before you go – have you got plenty of nappies packed for little Hamish?" and as she spoke she not only screwed her eyes up more tightly, but put a finger in her free ear, which was also the ear closest to Richard.

"Nappies! Oh, God!" cried Richard, beating his head against the wall, but not very hard.

"We'll be round right away," said Mrs Potter. "What? Oh, that's just Richard. He sends his love, and so do Daddy and Tycho."

"I don't!" Richard howled. "I wish Hudson would nail her foot to the floor. I don't want you, Africa! Stay where you belong!"

"She's very upset!" Mrs Potter said, turning from the phone. "Oh, Richard, dear – do believe me, my heart sank too. But she was so upset, I couldn't be hard on her."

"I knew it couldn't last," Mr Potter said, not without deep satisfaction.

"Did you hear?" Richard shouted, seeing Tycho walking towards them. "Africa!" he then exclaimed bitterly, without waiting for an answer. "She's leaving Hudson at two o'clock in the morning."

"Now, Richard, we don't know how serious it is," his mother said. "They've probably just had a lover's tiff."

"A lover's tiff?" Richard flung himself at the wall again, clawing it as if he were trying to climb straight up it like an infuriated cat. "Why do I stay in this house? Why – that's what I ask myself."

"And then you point out to yourself that you're out of work and dead broke," Tycho said.

"Oh yes, well, apart from that!" Richard replied, quite unabashed. Indeed, being reminded of his own unsatisfactory qualities seemed to restore him to good humour.

"You're only growing that beard because it's free," Tycho said, hoping to divert his father on to a lesser grievance, for Richard's beard was not yet sufficiently established to improve his appearance, and at that hour in the morning –

wearing an old caftan of Africa's which he had recently found at the dark end of her wardrobe and had taken to sleeping in – he looked like a dreadful, disordered, goatish parody of his older sister.

"I've got to have a hobby," Richard said. "It's the boredom and the drumming in the jungle! The drums! The drums!"

"I think you've both sent yourselves mad with some dreadful drug," Mr Potter said, glaring at them. He had always been puzzled and often irritated by the games that his children played so easily. "I'm getting the car out."

"Give her time to pack the nappies!" Tycho said. "Anyhow, it's out already. I didn't put it into the garage last night."

"Oh, Tycho!" said his mother reproachfully. "You know, dear, there are so many car thefts in the city these days..."

"It's a privilege that you're allowed to use the car the way you do," Mr Potter began, turning towards him sternly.

"Any car thief would only have to breathe on our garage door and it would fling itself open shouting, 'Take the car, but spare, spare me!'" Richard pointed out. He looked at Tycho disapprovingly. "You're being very cool about all this, I must say."

Tycho rolled his eyes, made a soft bubbling sound by pulling at his lower lip with his forefinger, but said nothing.

"Well, just bear in mind that if she comes back, bringing little Hamish with her, not to mention a million nappies, she'll want her old room back, and that's the room *I'm* in at present, so I'll have to move back to *my* old room, which is now *your* room, so we'll both be losers. Consider the logistics..."

"I know!" Tycho said. "I thought of that, first thing."

Their mother and father had vanished, no doubt intending to change into clothes suitable for reclaiming a weeping and recently married daughter at two o'clock in the morning. "I don't like it any more than you do," he said, "but you won't talk them out of it."

Richard accepted this with a sigh. He sat down in the hard, straight chair by the phone. Africa had never used it. Tycho could remember her sprawled right across their narrow hall, her long legs propped up on the wall. You had had to step over her to get from the hall to the kitchen.

"Why Africa?" he said. "Why on earth is she the favourite?"

"She was the oldest," Tycho suggested. "She's a girl... She has the advantage of being first." But he did not really know the answer.

"Richard, don't be so unkind!" called Mrs Potter from her bedroom. "I haven't got any favourites. If either of you rang me in tears at two a.m. and said that your husband had struck you, I'd be anxious to come and rescue you too."

"Struck her," groaned Richard. "It's the only sensible thing Hudson has ever done. But he must have messed it up as usual because she got to the phone, didn't she? I promise that if *I'd* have struck her she'd have stayed unconscious for hours."

"Domestic violence isn't a thing to joke about," Mr Potter said reprovingly, reappearing and looking remarkably spruce for a man who had been absent only a moment or two. He was wearing his best camel-hair dressing-gown, specially bought for a hospital visit some years ago, had knotted a white silk scarf at his throat and brushed his grey hair.

"Look at that! The Noel Coward of Ferry Road," said Richard, naming the road that would carry his parents between old houses and light industry to the flat of their distressed daughter. "I'm surprised you didn't put on full evening-dress and carry a cigarette-holder."

"Richard – you're being ridiculous," Mr Potter said, looking at himself in the hall mirror.

"Oo la la!" Richard retorted. "Look at him! He's preening himself!"

"Richard, I'm afraid you're beginning to sound jealous of your sister," Mr Potter said, quite unmoved.

"Of course I'm jealous," Richard said, "and so is Tycho, aren't you, Tyke? You've often wondered why he was so short. Well, I'll tell you now: it's jealousy that's stunted him."

"I tried to grow," Tycho said, responding immediately. "I did my best, but I was weighed down hour after hour by..."

His mother came out, completely dressed in the clothes she had worn earlier in the day.

"Are the keys in the kitchen, Tycho dear?" she asked. "You didn't leave the keys in the car, did you?" She smiled at her sons. "You do talk a lot of rubbish, you two," she said lovingly. "Richard, dear, don't worry, we'll work something out, but if you wouldn't mind just for the present moving back into Tycho's room..."

"I mind bitterly!" Richard said, and bared his teeth like a chimpanzee.

"You hide it so well though," Tycho added. "You're strong! Strong!"

The phone rang again and they all stood staring at it stupidly. Mrs Potter picked it up and they all heard the vibration of Africa's dramatic contralto once more. Mrs Potter listened intently. The voice went on and on. In the kitchen beyond her, Tycho could see Morris-the-cat (a deceptive animal who had been acquired as a tom kitten but who had undergone a dramatic sex change a few months later) taking up a position by the refrigerator. She looked up at it and began a loud purring.

"I'm so relieved," Mrs Potter said at last. "Darling, that's wonderful. Of course there's always a room for you here – you know that – but there's nothing like your own home." A moment later, after many promises of affection and messages to Hamish and even Hudson, she put the phone down.

"They've made it up again," she said. "He didn't exactly strike her – he just said he felt like it. You see, Richard – there was no need for all that fuss. Tycho didn't complain."

"He'd have complained tomorrow morning all right when that sexy schoolgirl witch he goes around with turned up and he had no room of his own," Richard said.

"It's morning now! She'll be here in six and a half hours," Tycho said, wondering with his own private kind of despair, just how it was that, having woken in the middle of a family crisis, and without consciously thinking about it, he had still worked out exactly how long it would be before he saw Angela May again. "All we do is talk about stars and books," he added in a bored voice.

"More fool you then!" said Richard. "I'll tell you now, a girl like Angela May wants a bit more than stars and books."

Yes, but not from me! Tycho said silently to himself, the words running round and round the domed attic of his head until, exhausted, they faded away to nothing.

"She doesn't want to be collected then?" Mr Potter said, talking of Africa, not Angela, slow to accept that he had changed dressing-gowns in the early hours of the morning for no real reason.

"No, dear! She says that she and Hudson have to work things out for themselves."

"It's worth the pain of fighting for the pleasure of making up afterwards," Tycho said. "That's what it says in books."

Angela would have known he was pinpointing yet another fine, old romantic notion, but all his mother said was, "I suppose that's true," though looking very doubtful as she agreed. "She's looking forward to seeing us all the night after tomorrow night. NO! It *is* tomorrow by now, isn't it?"

"Tomorrow night? Is she planning a return bout?" asked Richard.

"Oh, Richard!" cried his mother scornfully. "Wake up! It's their wedding anniversary. Don't you remember they're having a bit of a do to celebrate the first year. We're all invited."

"It'll be a bit like sitting up to see *On the Mat*," said Richard, naming a famous television programme on wrestling.

"Shall we club together and send a wreath?" Tycho asked him.

"Now, don't be cynical," Mrs Potter said mildly. "It doesn't suit either of you. Come on, dear," she added to her husband, who was stroking his own camel-hair sleeve, apparently consoling his dressing-gown for its disappointment. "We've got to catch up on some sleep."

She seldom joined in the exchanges of smart remarks with which Richard, Tycho and Africa used to entertain themselves, but she had a soft way of having the last word, due, no doubt, to years of practice. Her sons went to their separate rooms, glad that they were not being forced to share after all. Within a few moments the house was as quiet and restful as it had been before the interruption, and Morris-the-cat, realising the fridge would not be opened just yet, curled up in a carton of cleaning rags beside it and went to sleep too.

3

FAMILY MATTERS

When Tycho woke later it was proper morning, but getting up all over again had a strange, dream-like feel about it as if there were a fault in time, which meant he was doomed to do the same thing over and over again. He woke up, looking at his wall pinned with quotations, then turned slowly over. On the floor beside his bed lay a thick, dark-covered book he had been looking through the night before, *The Catalogue of the Universe*, a birthday present from Angela herself.

As he turned, the door opened and Richard came into his room, because many of his clothes were still in the big chest of drawers he and Tycho had shared for many years. Africa's old room was tiny and Richard, who had collected odd clothes from junk shops and school fairs for seven years now, could not fit them all in, though he had added on to the wardrobe with a piece of clothes line, cuphooks and a plastic shower curtain with a picture of Marilyn Monroe on it. Ten minutes later, Tycho, half-dressed in faded but very tidy blue jeans, watched his brother curiously as he put on the skin-tight scarlet skivvy, and then over that an equally tight blue one full of holes gaping like mouths, letting the scarlet throats show from beneath. Richard's jeans were dirty and frayed around all their edges and were patched with triangles and squares of flowery velvet, bright yellow canvas and pink plastic. Over all this he wore a jerkin that appeared to have been knitted from sky-blue rope. He rejoiced in being unkempt and unironed but, for all that, he took far more care over his appearance than Tycho did. Finished himself, it was his turn to watch Tycho who was carefully putting lotion in the bend of his arm.

"I didn't know you went in for after-shave," Richard said in surprise. "Why there?"

"It's for the allergy," Tycho explained.

At this time of year he suffered from hayfever and sometimes a rash appeared along with it. Tycho thought of it written down like a supermarket promise, *Take hayfever this month and get a free rash as well.* For in some ways the world was like a shopping centre and he himself was a doubtful customer, often ineffectual, being talked into buying things he didn't want, things indeed which nobody in their right mind would buy.

"Good old Tyke! Nothing's easy for you, is it?" Richard said, sitting down on the bed that had once been his, at the moment piled with washing waiting to be sorted out into things that had to be ironed and things that could go directly to their cupboards and drawers.

"Bloody Africa!" Richard then said. He desperately wanted someone to sympathise with him over the threat of Africa's return.

"Never mind! It didn't happen!" Tycho said, opening his own drawer and taking out a T-shirt. His drawer was extremely neat, things folded precisely and placed in piles. "Not this time, anyhow."

"What do you mean, 'Not this time'?" Richard demanded. "Do you know something I don't?"

He looked frantic at the thought of missing out on vital family information.

"No," Tycho replied, laughing at him. "It's just that she's almost certain to come home sooner or later. I can't believe she'll stay married to Hudson, can you – honestly? And where will she go except back here, with Mum as a built-in babysitter?"

The truth of this made Richard silent as he assessed his chances of finding somewhere cheap to live before this prophecy was fulfilled.

"It's not right!" he said at last. "Mum should be getting out and doing something else, enjoying herself a bit more. Dad too! They've brought up their family and they should be allowed to get on to the next bit. Goodness knows they haven't had much fun what with Dad's trouble."

Tycho had nothing to add to this. He thought Richard was right, but he could not help seeing that in many ways his parents really wanted Africa back again. She was his father's darling, and his mother adored little Hamish who was pretty and amusing and, on the whole, a good baby. Africa had always been difficult and demanding and as a result their lives were founded on her. Once gone, she could not be replaced.

"It wouldn't matter if we had a house that was twice as big," Richard went on.

"We're lucky to have this one," Tycho couldn't help saying.

Mr Potter had been involved in a car accident when Tycho was a baby. A carelessly driven car had knocked him off a bicycle. He had been in hospital with head injuries and severe concussion, but the damage had not seemed to be permanent. He came home from hospital and life went on much as before for a little while. However, some time later, at a parents' evening at the school, Mr Potter had fallen down in front of other parents beside the Room Six handwork table in the dramatic first of a series of fits, and after that the life of the Potter family was changed for ever.

Tycho could not remember this occasion, but he knew its effect had been terrible. Mr Potter was left permanently guilty over an imperfection that was not his fault and that proved to be almost entirely controllable by drugs (though he was never allowed to drive the family car again and, when he worked in the garden, any long silence would bring one or other of the family out to check up on him). Africa felt guilty too, because she had been so deeply ashamed of him for a while that he had never recovered from the shock of her childish resentment. Mrs Potter had learned to cope, Richard had never seemed to care very much, treating his father as though he were the same man he had always been, while the troubles of Mr Potter, misunderstood as they often were, were visited on Tycho in a curious way which none of his family had ever completely acknowledged. After all, there was nothing anyone could do about it.

Perhaps the truest and most serious injury of all, far more serious than the original epilepsy, was the alteration not only in Mr Potter's view of himself, but in the changed attitude his employers took of him. "Cannot cope with stress," it said on his personal report.

In a way this was true or came to be true, which might just as well have been the same thing. From what Tycho could understand, his father had closed down in many ways, had given up his government job and had stopped trying to cope with stress at all, except now and then where Africa was concerned. He had a job as groundsman at a workers' educational establishment next to the shopping centre half a block away. Mrs Potter worked three days a week in a fancy goods shop, and took china-painting classes at the very place where her husband was employed. Since he could not drive and she did not care to, on the whole their lives were circumscribed by the pleasant, unadventurous streets around them. Their battles with the wider world were all conducted through stormy Africa or through Richard, who chose to violate every precept they had concerning how people should look, speak and particularly how they should behave to parents.

Now Richard watched as Tycho, self-conscious but obstinate, pinned up another piece of paper over his bed.

"What's that?" he asked suspiciously and, when Tycho did not answer, came briskly across the room to read it for himself.

"Nothing exists but atoms and the void," he read in Tycho's careful, italic writing, and then turned on his brother with a sort of fury. "God, you're so affected!" he cried. "Does it make you feel good, sticking up something some old Greek said a million years ago, instead of a picture of a heavy rock band. You're so damned middle-class!"

This was Richard's great term of abuse.

"Yes, and it's my middle-class room and my middle-class bed," Tycho exclaimed. "If I'd stuck it up over your bed you'd have something to growl about. It struck me as a thing to think about. I mean Democritus said that in 430 BC." Richard stared at him blankly. "430 BC," Tycho repeated, as if he expected Richard to be somehow moved by this fact. Richard pulled a face and Tycho turned away impatiently.

"If you think your girlfriend's going to be impressed by this junk, you're wrong," Richard said, idly picking up one of the weights Tycho used in a vague effort to make himself stronger. "You'd better concentrate on the weight-lifting – not that it will make you any taller," he added. "Give up hope on that one!"

"She's not my girlfriend!" Tycho said. "Just a good friend who comes to call."

"Oh sure!" Richard said. "Now I'll tell you something! Any girl like Angela May is never, ever under any circumstances just anyone's good friend..." He hesitated and added, "Particularly not of a boy who once had *The Joy of Sex* hidden in a drawer under a jersey."

"I liked the pictures," Tycho said, crossing his eyes and then turning his back on Richard. He began to set out the things he might need for the day ahead, concentrating on method and order, but all the same he felt himself beginning to blush at the memory of his mother spring-cleaning the week before Africa's wedding, straightening every drawer in the house as if Africa's new in-laws might slip into the bedrooms and check them out.

"What on earth is *this*," she had cried, holding up *The Joy of Sex* in front of Richard, who still shared the room in those days. Sometimes it seemed that Richard's hoot of derision still echoed there. Even his mother, who had been apologetic at accidentally betraying him, was also amused.

Tycho set out his wallet with some money and his driving licence in it, a paperback novel, a ring-backed notebook with a blue pen and a green pen clipped to the cover. He did not want to admit to Richard that Angela was not only a good friend but a continual torment, which he had learned to live with rather as he lived with hayfever and its allergy bonus. "Oh well, everyone thinks Angela's sexy," he said, as if he were only vaguely interested. "But there's no point in thinking about it, is there? Her boyfriends are all terrific—" He paused and added, "Full-backs and fast-bowlers and so on. I'm just not her type. OK?"

"Don't be so wet!" Richard cried. "Get shot of all these ancient Greeks. Do a bit of weight-lifting, take a dose of deer velvet, go up to her, take her in your arms, and say... say..." Richard hesitated.

"Here is your desert lover," Tycho suggested suddenly.

"What?" Richard was momentarily distracted.

"What I want I take!" Tycho declared powerfully, and began to laugh. "But I haven't got any monogrammed Turkish cigarettes."

"What are you babbling about?" Richard said crossly, and Tycho relented.

"It's in an old book, *The Sheik*," he explained. "Remember Rudolph Valentino?"

"That's an old film," Richard said suspiciously.

"It's a book too. Angela lent it to me," Tycho said. "The hero was like a graceful, cruel, merciless beast and smoked monogrammed Turkish cigarettes."

"He sounds as if he was a closet gay," Richard declared. "Listen, if it's as hopeless as all that, why does she bother to visit you?"

"It just has to be for the grandeur of my mind," Tycho said, shaking his head.

"The grandeur of your mind!" Richard cried. "I was just as bright at school as you. I couldn't be bothered going along with all that fascist organisation, that's all."

"You call anything that involves work 'fascist'," Tycho retorted. "Don't go taking it out on me because you're frightened Africa might come back again and sling you out of her room. I'm getting sick of all this."

"Breakfast, boys!" their mother called from the kitchen, but neither of them moved immediately; Richard, because he was reminded of Africa and his fragile hold on a piece of private space, Tycho, because having started the morning all lucid and in control, he now felt like a pool grown clouded and muddy because someone had stirred it up with a pointed stick. He needed time to settle and grow clear again.

It was hard for Tycho to give any account of why Angela came to visit him, because when they were apart he was not always sure himself. It was true that he had the use of a car, but Angela was often allowed to use her own mother's car, particularly in the evenings, and anyway she could easily have begged lifts from half-a-dozen other people during the day. No one else would believe it, but he believed that she too enjoyed struggling with the mystery of a mysterious world, and his own advantage was his power to detect, not answers perhaps, but clues that might lead to answers. He wondered if he was so wrong in thinking that Angela liked him because he chased these elusive clues through fairy tales, novels, romances, accounts of the behaviour of birds, of chromosomes or quarks. Through amazing facts, the voices of matter, time and even of the void spoke to him, begging for introductions to beautiful girls.

"Angela May, may I present Planck's Constant. Energy is not continuous, but comes in small discrete units. How does that grab you?" He saw the word *discrete* spelt *discreet* and imagined quantums of energy posted out in plain wrappers, like a series of dirty books.

"Breakfast, dear!" called his mother.

"Breakfast, dear!" called Richard, waving a hand at him. "Come on! Snap out of it. I'll tell you this," he added generously to Tycho, "I wouldn't mind taking her on if you give up."

"Who?" asked Tycho, pretending to be confused – quite easy for he almost was. Richard looked at him with needle eyes, but simply said as they went into the hall, "Mum doesn't like her, you know." Tycho did know, and for months had wondered why. For it seemed to him that Angela had a great deal in common with Africa, but perhaps there was a certain relief for his mother in being able to dislike Africa's qualities in someone who was not a daughter.

Richard slouched down the hall in his boneless way. "You're so damned neat," he said. "You're so *tight*! I can't see why Mum and Dad don't give up on Africa as family favourite and have you instead."

"She's Dad's favourite, maybe, but I don't think Mum has favourites – not really," Tycho said, following him. "I mean Mum's like some birds. Whichever chick makes the loudest noise – that's the one she feeds. That's why weaker chicks just die off in some species," he added in an impersonal voice. "They can't call out loudly enough and they don't get fed. There are some Australian falcons that start off with four chicks and only raise one or two…"

"Here endeth the first lesson!" Richard interrupted, referring to Tycho's habit of automatically passing on information.

"Sorry!" Tycho said, as they went into the kitchen.

Discovering that few people were amazed by wonderful pieces of information made up one of two big dislocations in Tycho's life. The other was the discovery, when he was quite a small boy, that people thought he was ugly, and that this often prevented them from liking him. He remembered very vividly a woman, whom he did not know, speaking pleasantly to his mother as they walked together into a supermarket, staring hard at him as she did so. "What a very unfortunate child that youngest Potter boy is," he heard her say a moment later to another acquaintance. She must have realised, if she had thought about it, that Tycho was close enough to hear her, but perhaps she thought that, being so much taller than he was, she could speak in a normal voice and go unheard. Or perhaps she did not care. "Has he got the same trouble as his father? He doesn't look quite normal!"

His high, round forehead with the fine hair lying on it as limp and soft as white feathers, his high cheek bones and snub nose had certainly made an odd-looking child of him.

"You're a changeling!" Africa had once told him in a fit of irritation. "What with you and Dad in the family, I just don't know how I survive."

"It's a lovely morning," Mrs Potter said cheerfully. "How nice you both look."

"Since we look the dead opposite of one another," Richard began.

"...in your different ways," Mrs Potter finished, giving Richard a triumphant glance.

"Richard, the whole hall reeks of that incense you burn," Mr Potter said sternly.

"Oh, yes," Richard said vaguely, sitting down and shaking muesli lavishly from the packet into his bowl.

"I hope you don't think I'm fooled by it. I know it's there

41

to hide something else," Mr Potter went on in a knowing voice. "I mightn't be what you would call 'trendy' but I..."

"Do you think I've had women in there?" Richard asked, growing alert and defensive at once. "I haven't, but even if I had, so what? You're not the Lord God watching over the Garden of Eden, you know."

Mr Potter managed to suggest, with a single, bitter smile, that if he had been watching over the Garden of Eden a great deal of subsequent trouble would have been averted.

"I did not mean that!" he said with calm dignity. "I did think perhaps you had been smoking something not quite..."

"Perish the thought!" cried Richard, casting up his eyes. "Defile the room that little Hamish was probably conceived in. Father, you do me wrong!"

"Dear, that's not very nice," Mrs Potter said comfortably. "Poor little chap!"

Richard, who had certainly not intended any insult to his baby nephew, was momentarily puzzled into silence. Tycho met his mother's eyes briefly, and she gave him one of her funny winks, screwing up the left side of her face for the fraction of a second, as if she had confused Richard on purpose, and perhaps she had.

Mr Potter, anxious to avoid any consideration of Hamish's beginnings, looked at Richard's beard and sighed deeply.

"I suppose it's no use my saying anything..." he began, which usually meant he was going to have quite a lot to say.

Tycho was actually in his room when he saw Angela's red hair pass his window like a shooting star.

"Angela," he heard his mother cry cheerfully in the kitchen. "Lovely to see you."

"How about a cup of coffee with a dear old man?" Mr Potter said invitingly.

"No, thank you!" Angela replied. "Actually I've had two cups already this morning." She was always very polite to Tycho's parents and particularly to his mother, because she half-suspected they did not approve of her, and teased them with manners so good they were beyond criticism.

"Tycho did say he'd be able to give me a lift again today," Angela now said, explaining her presence, even though she had been expected.

"Of course, dear! He's in his room. You know the way," said Mrs Potter. Her kindly tolerance sounded quite genuine. Only Tycho's practised ear could detect the strain.

("I don't think she's altogether fair to you boys, dressing the way she does," she had said two days earlier, referring to Angela's shorts, which had been very short indeed.)

Tycho waited with anticipation and alarm to see what she might be wearing today.

"What's Tycho got that I haven't?" asked Mr Potter jovially. Richard was right. He often became flirtatious in a fatherly way when Angela came calling.

"A telescope and mysterious thoughts, or that's what he says!" Richard yelled from his room. "Don't be so fatuous, you old goat!"

"That disembodied voice you hear is my oldest son," Mr Potter said with spirit. "His mother says he was a dear little

43

boy once, and she's an honest woman on the whole, so I suppose he must have been."

"That's quite good," Richard cried encouragingly. "Go on in and see Tyke, Angela, before my old man comes over all winsome again."

The moment Tycho saw Angela he knew she was excited about something. It was easy to recognise her planning mood. Though he passed on information freely, he often closed down around new ideas like a sea anemone wrapping itself around prey, digesting them secretly, sharing them with almost no one except his mother – when he could get her undivided attention – and, over the past two years, with Angela herself. Sometimes, as he talked, he would find her looking at him, as a small child might watch its first magician, and this intense stare made him feel as if he might actually succeed in breaking out of his baffling chrysalis some day, and become – nothing as sunny as a butterfly – but a velvet moth of darkness with feathery antennae and moons on his deep wings. Angela on the other hand was a daytime person and when she had an idea she wore it openly, displayed it, sometimes without naming it, and polished it in front of everyone. If it was a truly good idea it crackled in her like electricity, right out to the ends of her hair, or ran just under her skin and made her burn. She was burning now.

"What's up?" he asked curiously.

"Nothing!" she said, and added, "Well, nothing much."

"OK, keep your secrets!" Tycho said. "See if I care."

"I'll tell you later – but not yet," she promised. "There *is* something but – hey, Tyke – let's get out of this community-service thing. Exams are over and they can't expel us, can they? And even if they did, there's only one day of real school left. Ten out of ten for style if we wound up getting expelled on the last day!"

Tycho did not think there would be any glory in it, just embarrassment and nagging and disappointment at home.

"Robin wouldn't be all that thrilled if you got expelled," he pointed out. He would have enjoyed hating Robin for some good reason, but Robin was thoroughly pleasant and Tycho was reduced to ordinary, despicable jealousy, and even that was tired and passive.

"Oh, well – Robin's got to learn to take the rough with the smooth," Angela said, looking in Tycho's mirror and playing with her short, crinkly hair, pushing it away from her forehead, apparently admiring the deep arrow of the widow's peak that so noticeably marked her forehead. She half-closed her eyes, fluttered her eyelashes at herself, and pouted her lips, making a face of filmstar passion, and then, turning, gave him a look that was inviting him to be amused at her gesticulations. Once, earlier in the year, she had turned from this very mirror and looked at him, standing in the room behind her clutching *The Catalogue of the Universe* (which she had just given him as a birthday present) as if it were a lover, or a shield.

"Come on, Big Science! How about it?" she had said in a strange voice, kind, curious, yet breathless too. Tycho was overwhelmed by the moment and the offer. She was offering to let him kiss her and touch her, which he did, prepared to give himself up to her, but then he accidentally saw himself in the mirror, as much embraced as embracing, and a terrible cupboard in his memory burst open, scattering a thousand stored-up slights and insults through his head. All he could think was that he looked ridiculous and made love seem ridiculous, and somehow lessened Angela, whereas someone like Robin enhanced her. Angela had laughed, thinking he was merely shy, inviting him to laugh too. Then she had grown confused by his self-consciousness, and at last hurt and scornful. The memory of his rapidly stepping back from her and turning away hung between them like the memory of a shared failure, but just what sort of failure and on whose part, it was difficult to tell. Yet Angela was still calling on him, wearing tight jeans and thin, floppy shirts made of cheesecloth, the sleeves rolled up, and socks and sneakers because, though the day was warm, they had been told not to wear mere sandals, for the work ahead involved chopping and slicing rough stems of bracken and gorse.

"You could lose a toe if you're not careful, so do be sensible," the teacher had said. And Angela was being as sensible as her limited range of footwear allowed her.

"Let's give the gorse-cutting a miss," she tempted him. "*Gone With the Wind* is on for positively the last time this century at the Academy."

"Frankly, Scarlett, I don't give a damn!" Tycho said. "We've seen it twice."

"My dear!" Angela corrected him. "Rhett Butler said, 'Frankly, my dear. . .'"

"Let's save our money for the Humphrey Bogart festival next month," Tycho suggested.

"But we've seen *Casablanca* twice too," Angela said. "Oh well, here's looking at you, kid."

And she *was* looking at him, very speculatively.

"I thought I might have to rescue you from my old man," Tycho said. "I heard him getting all – all roguish out there."

"Oh well, I don't mind," Angela said amiably. "It's sort of flattering. Are you ready to go? You must be! You look like Christopher Robin going for an interview at a missionary college. Come on! Be a devil. Rumple your hair a bit!" She proceeded to do this for him.

"It's not flattering – it's embarrassing," Tycho grumbled, smoothing his hair with his hand. "My father, I mean."

"You only worry because he is your father," Angela said indifferently. "There's a lot of things you can put up with, as long as you're not related to them."

"Lucky you! Having only one parent halves the risk!" Tycho said.

Angela looked up. She had very dark eyes fringed with long thick lashes. At this moment they were dense and unreadable.

"At least you know the worst about yours," she said lightly. "I've got to wonder."

"Big deal!" Tycho picked up his pack, and slung it over his shoulder. "Well, mine aren't too bad really," he said, relenting.

"It's just that we're on top of each other the whole time. Let's hit the road."

"Tyke!" Angela said, stopping him with the tone of her voice. There she stood, his bed and Democritus on one side of her, the spare bed and the unsorted washing on the other, poised either to ask an important question or to disclose a secret.

"What?" he asked apprehensively. She hesitated, and then changed her mind again.

"Oh, I'll tell you later after all," she said. "Not now!"

They were standing face to face, quite close to each other, and Tycho was reminded, regretfully, that she was taller than he was. Mr Potter, stalking past, looked in, saw them and thumped on the hall panelling.

"Come on now! Break it up!" he cried in his bounciest voice.

"There's nothing to break up!" Tycho shouted back, intensely irritated, and heard Richard bound triumphantly out into the hall.

"God – do you realise what *damage* he's doing to us?" Richard shouted to his mother in the kitchen. "If Tyke and I ever get married, which God forbid, we'll spend our wedding nights sitting on the edge of a motel bed somewhere, cowering and waiting for him to bang on the door and shout, 'Come on! Break it up.'"

"Oh, do stop it, you two!" cried Mrs Potter wearily. "I get so sick of it all! And what will Angela think?"

"I don't think anything – honestly," Angela said. But she

looked fascinated, which did not reassure Mrs Potter who naturally wanted her family to seem perfect to all outsiders.

"Let's get out!" said Tycho. "And then they'll be able to have a good quarrel without us around."

"I hope you've thanked your mother for letting you have the car," Mr Potter was moved to say. "It is the family car, you know."

"Yes, I have," said Tycho. "But I'll do it again if you like. Thanks, Mum!"

"It's quite all right, I wasn't using it today..." Mrs Potter began, but Richard flung himself forward saying, "You haven't done it properly, Tyke!" Then he fell on his knees before his mother, seized her hand and began smothering it with kisses. "Oh, thank you, dearest Mother, for lending me your clapped-out mini! Thank you with my hand on my pounding heart. I know Dad's work is just down the road and yours is only half a block away. I know you have no possible use for the car today, but thank you – thank you – thank you..."

"Out!" said Tycho, desperately seizing the keys from their hook over the sink, and he and Angela fled to the sound of Richard's babbled "*thank yous*", Angela laughing and looking back over her shoulder.

The mini was parked in the drive. Tycho and Angela threw their packs into the back, scrambled into the car after them and slammed the doors. However, Mrs Potter came after them, calling to Tycho and holding a package in her hand.

"You forgot your lunch!" she said through the open window.

"Mum, you didn't have to!" Tycho exclaimed. "I can cut my own lunch. Or even buy it."

"Oh well, a little treat!" Mrs Potter said. "And don't forget Africa's present, will you? Nothing big – just something."

Beyond her, Morris-the-cat lay down on the warm concrete and began rolling and patting the air with her paws, loving the day, relaxed and easy in her soft fur coat.

"Your mother's a really motherly sort of woman," Angela said, half-sighing as Tycho backed the car down the drive – two strips of concrete set in closely clipped lawn. "But why does she look at me so suspiciously? Does she think I'm out to *get* you – marry you for your scholarship (if you get it that is) and your pen that writes in eight colours?"

Tycho leaned briefly on the horn, warning pedestrians and cyclists that a car was about to shoot out on to the public road.

"You've forgotten my telescope," he said, "and my collection of quotations. You could do a heck of a lot worse."

"But why doesn't she like me?" Angela persisted. "I can just feel she doesn't."

"Yes, she does," said Tycho, lying, "but you probably seem a bit high-powered – dangerous even. You know what parents are like, always thinking safe and happy come to the same thing where their kids are concerned." His own parents had certainly felt that about Africa. He swung the car on to the road. "Or maybe 'safe' means less trouble for a parent. I don't know," he added, looking into the rear-mirror.

"But *you're* safe!" Angela exclaimed, half-mockingly as she snapped her seat belt on. "Terribly safe! Safe from me, anyway!"

"I haven't much choice," Tycho said. "Don't take it out on me."

Angela frequently said unexpected things, and she said one of them now. "Never mind! I *honour* you, Big Science, in spite of everything." She laughed, pleased at his startled expression.

"What do you mean – in spite of everything?" Tycho said quickly. "You mean *because* of everything – that's what you really mean in your heart of hearts."

"I don't!" Angela said. "I mean in spite of your dreadful hair and the fact that you dress like some country-and-western fan. OK – I know I sling off at you a bit because you do get accidentally pompous if someone doesn't bring you back into line, but I know you're brilliant in your own little way."

"I'd rather be tall," Tycho said.

"At least be thankful!" Angela said. "There's plenty of people short and stupid with it. You could be much worse off, couldn't you?"

And this was certainly true.

4

THE WOBBLE IN THE CEMETERY OF THE WORLD

"I think that's it!" said the supervising teacher. "The rest of the day's your own." There were cheers from his pupils. Tycho saw Angela look at her watch and go to speak to Robin.

"I'm heading off with Tyke," he heard her say. "I'll meet you at the Gladstone car park later on, usual time, and don't you dare be late."

"I'll collect you," Robin said. "I can manage Dry Creek Road – no sweat!"

"I don't want Dido to think people will call for me, or she mightn't ever let me have the car again," Angela said quickly. "I'll drive down."

Tycho, at Angela's elbow, knew, however, that there was a big piece of Angela's life that did not match up with Robin's. She did not want Robin to find out that she lived in a house with an outside lavatory.

Angela's home consisted of two Ministry-of-Works cottages placed side by side making four rooms in all, with a lean-to bathroom tacked on to the end. The whole improvisation was linked together with an attractive verandah, once part of a grander house, but which, with its posts cut down a little, fitted 1000 Dry Creek Road surprisingly well. All the same, though it made a home it did not make a house. At the end of an uneven brick path stood the outside lavatory, utterly necessary but a little disgraceful. Angela did not want Robin to have to negotiate this path, or to see the spade and the tin of chemical revealing that, once a week either Dido or Angela herself had to dig a hole and empty a can. It was not that Angela was ashamed of her funny home, but rather that she loved it and wanted to protect it from being patronised.

"Catch up with you later then," Robin said. "We'll check out this Dunedin band. See you around, Tyke."

"Anyone need a lift back?" asked the supervising teacher, but Tycho and Angela had their own transport and watched first Robin and then the school minibus drive off down the hill without them. On the opposite spur they could make out if they wanted to the long, stony scar of the dry creek, and the cluster of trees that hid 1000 Dry Creek Road.

"Where's Rob off to?" Tycho asked idly.

"He's got to help his father in the factory," Angela said.

"Oh gosh, the poor old rich!" cried Tycho rather sourly. "We don't realise how they suffer."

"Just as well," Angela said, "because I want to do something really special this afternoon and I don't want him along."

"Empty the loo!" suggested Tycho, and Angela grinned, and thumped his arm so that the top half of it gave a painful, electrical thrill and went numb.

"It's mad!" she said. "He'd put up with all sorts of things, but I just think he'd run a mile if he saw our house properly in the daylight – not to mention my dear old, grey-haired mum. He'd have second thoughts about me. Third ones too probably. You wouldn't think so, but Rob's a bit of an old woman deep down."

Tycho couldn't help enjoying these comments which were almost criticisms of Robin.

"There's nothing wrong with Dido," he argued, rubbing his upper arm.

"Nothing *wrong*!" Angela said dubiously. "Nothing actually wrong, but she's a bit weird."

"Eccentrics are OK socially," Tycho told her. "Perfectly acceptable, my dear."

"Yes, well, that's part of the trouble," Angela grumbled. "It's not as if she's a real eccentric. I mean she's not what I'd call colourful. It is more as if she was on loan from another planet, almost like ours but not quite – a sort of near miss. What with her and you, I'm stuck with a couple of freaks. You weren't the only one awake at two o'clock this morning. I was up too because the moon was so bright, and there was Dido outside in dressing-gown and gumboots scything the grass."

"There's nothing wrong with that," Tycho said, after a pause.

"There's nothing altogether right about it either," Angela replied. "It was really spooky to look out and see her there. Isn't there some sort of crab that behaves in a certain way at high tide, and even if you take it away from its home, it still goes on doing its high-tide things according to the beach it came from? You told me about it once. Well, it was as if Dido was acting according to high tide in another dimension."

"Is that what you were going to tell me about?" Tycho asked. "You know – you said this morning you were going to tell me something."

"The thing is, if I tell you now you might try and talk me out of it, and I can't be bothered with common sense," Angela said. "I'd rather present you with a – a – what's that thing people get presented with, and they can't get out of it once they've got it."

"A retirement present?" Tycho guessed, frowning.

"A *fait accompli*!" Angela cried triumphantly. "I want to present you with one of those. I've already engraved your name on it."

"Well, where do you want to go?" Tycho asked.

"Nowhere just yet," Angela replied. "It's too early. We'll scramble around a bit. Did you know your nose is sunburnt?"

"Is it?" Tycho said. "I thought it was just on fire. Why don't you get sunburnt? I thought red-headed people always did."

"I do, at the beginning of the season," Angela said, "but after that I just tan. I'm lucky I suppose. My skin doesn't match up with my hair."

Like many lucky people, she somehow sounded slightly complacent as if, deep down, the good luck was something she really deserved.

They wandered along the community walk-track they had cleared during the morning and early afternoon, congratulating themselves on its new neatness and accessibility. Then they left the track and scrambled down into a shadowy gully under native fuschia and beech trees to find a little stream making a tiny, musical whisper as it slid casually through a tunnel of green ferns. It descended in a series of narrow basins, penetrated by arrows of sunlight, which turned the water, already darkened by rotting leaves, into pools of dusky gold. From these pools their reflections looked back at them, dark and featureless. Angela gazed into the stream half-enchanted, and Tycho up into the sky where the clouds continually melted and tore apart, hounded by the winds of the upper air. Electrified, he saw one cloud open an eye and look at him. A lid of white mist thinned and rolled back, and the eye, clear, blue and pupil-less, stared at him, as if he were the single thing it had been instructed to study. "You!" it seemed to command him. "Look into me – into me."

Tycho began to think he had often felt the pressure of that gaze, and was pleased to see it openly revealed. Mostly the heavens pretended to be blind. Unexpectedly he found himself blurting out something he had always been too deeply ashamed of to mention to anyone except his mother.

"You know – when I was a little kid people used to think I was subnormal!" he said. "Partly, well, I suppose I looked as if I came from another planet – but it was partly because of Dad. I mean a lot of people knew there was something wrong with him without knowing what, and anything like that scares them off."

He waited rather tensely for Angela to make a comment.

"No one who knew you could think that," she said.

"Yes, but they didn't want to get as far as knowing me," Tycho said. "You didn't, for instance. Whereas everyone wanted to know you."

Angela pulled a face and nodded, feeling a little pain in her heart on behalf of a younger Tycho whom she could never hope to comfort now.

"I can't do anything about it," she said. "It's just the way things are, Big Science."

"Oh, I know," Tycho agreed. "I'm not getting at you. And understanding it is a sort of relief. It's getting to the point where you *do* understand it – that's the hard bit." The eye in the sky was slowly pulling out of shape and becoming just a ragged hole in the clouds. "I did complain to my mother once," he said, "and she couldn't do anything either. She just told me to laugh it off and said, 'You know it's not true, that's the main thing.' OK – I suppose it was, but it didn't seem the main thing at the time."

Angela took a last look at her dark reflection and stood up, half-stretching. "It's not *fair*, though!" she exclaimed sternly. "Don't go all passive about it. Do whatever you can do."

"I don't need to worry now," Tycho said. "Anyhow, I wasn't passive even then. I tried to show people straight off I wasn't silly by telling them things I'd read, and they stopped thinking I was stupid and just thought I was a real pain."

Angela paused, brushing a few dead leaves and papery scraps of fuschia bark from her jeans.

"What's brought this on?" she asked curiously. "It's like a confession." Tycho did not know. "Maybe the creek muttering along makes you mutter too," she suggested. "You're copying nature."

"Could be," Tycho agreed. "Or it might be the effect of the big eye in the air!" However, the eye was now narrowing, disappearing while he looked up at it, probably having seen all it needed to see. "Actually, I began by thinking about you trying to keep your outside lavatory a secret from Robin. Why should it matter? It's not common sense. Still I know it does. The thing is, common sense and truth don't match – not all the time."

"That's absolutely like you – to say a thing like that!" Angela said vigorously. "Come on back to the car and tell me as we go."

"Common sense is tidy and truth's untidy," Tycho declared, following her obediently, but though he sounded certain of what he was saying, he was actually working something out. He was really talking to himself. "Common sense is very neat, and it's easy to see, and it's sort of symmetrical, bowling along in the open and looking completely real, but it's only common sense – whereas actual truth wobbles and hides."

"Wobbles and hides, wobbles and hides!" chanted Angela, smiling back at him. "You've invented a chorus! Wobbling, hiding truth."

"Truth's *furtive*," Tycho shouted up at her, beginning to enjoy his ideas, all the more because he believed them, and putting them into words gave him power over them.

"It's an ellipse, not a circle!" Angela cried back, catching his ideas, inspired by a story Tycho had once told her about Kepler working for years and years to define the orbit of Mars, constantly held up because he believed the orbit of the planet must be a circle. It had seemed so logical for it to be a circle with the sun at its centre, but Mars had tricked him by moving in a slight ellipse. "It's got two focuses," Angela said, remembering.

Tycho was thrilled with this idea.

"Spot on!" he said, stopping in his tracks. "The world's left-handed. Planets move in ellipses, parity isn't preserved, and the square root of two is an irrational number."

"That's right! Hit me with the heavy stuff!" grumbled Angela, scrambling on ahead of him. "I'll stick with ellipses. What was that about the square root of two?"

"It was a guilty secret of Pythagoras..."

"...the triangle man?" Angela asked, stopping at last.

"...the author of that bestselling theorem that's gone into hundreds of editions," Tycho nodded.

"Oh, *that* Pythagoras!" Angela continued to stare half-mockingly at Tycho. She was much further up the slope than he was and seemed to tower over him, but at that moment Tycho didn't care.

"He loved rational numbers – Pythagoras, that is. He desperately wanted the world to be symmetrical," he said exuberantly. "But the square root of two is an irrational number. It goes on for ever and never ends. It's untidy. Pythagoras tried to keep it a secret, but word got round. And some time in the nineteen-fifties a Chinese scientist..."

"Fu Man Chu!" Angela interrupted him, with a shout of laughter.

"Almost!" Tycho agreed, pulling himself two or three steps up after her. "It was a woman, I think..." The name came rushing out of memory. "Madam Wu!" he exclaimed triumphantly.

"Whooooo!" hooted Angela, stopping again, but Tycho stood transfixed below her, and slowly her own expression changed. Only the night before her mother's head had seemed to leak moonshine, now Tycho's seemed as if it might shine in a different way with his own sort of revelation.

"There was a cobalt nucleus," Tycho said. "Cobalt 60, I think. Anyhow, whatever it is, it's more likely to fling out an electron at the south end than the north. There you are! It's like a sort of wobble right in the very heart of the heart. It's not absolutely symmetrical. It just seems as if it ought to be."

"So – what's the big deal about symmetry after all?" Angela asked, though she knew the answer even as she asked the question. Tycho bounded up beside her. His sunburnt nose shone like a Christmas decoration, the centrepiece of a face alight with some enormous feeling. It was as if Tycho had been suddenly set free to be completely happy.

"The big deal is we're made to expect symmetry," he said. "We're satisfied by it when we see it. We look for it and when we see it we say, 'Terrific. There it is!' But we're wrong. Our idea of things being fair is a sort of symmetry, but there's always the wobble."

"The ellipse!" Angela insisted. "I like the word 'ellipse'. It's sort of silky."

For a moment she thought Tycho was going to put his arms around her and kiss her, looking up at her with an expression so soft, unguarded and powerful it could only be called passionate, but then he hesitated, his intensity faded and unexpectedly he touched his nose.

"It's not golden," he said. "The real Tycho's was golden. Mine's just sunburnt."

"You're the real Tycho," Angela said impatiently. "I hate it when you say you're not. Come on or we'll be late."

"What for?" asked Tycho cautiously.

"A wobble in the cemetery of the world," Angela said.

"Symmetry!" Tycho corrected her.

"Look, I know what I said." Angela stared down at him indignantly. "Though it's turned out cleverer than I meant it to be, now I come to think of it," she added thoughtfully. "Write it down and pin it up over your bed, Anthony Tycho Potter."

"I'll write it down as soon as I get back to the car," Tycho said. "I expect a lot of the best things are said by a sort of accident. Where do we go from here?"

5

ENCOUNTERS IN A CHANGING STREET

Directed by Angela, Tycho drove into town, parked the car and fed the meter with five-cent pieces. They were in a street where people had once come to shop, and indeed some of the old shops were still there, hanging on in an insecure and seedy fashion, even the new stock in their windows looking out-of-date and unwanted. All around them the street was changing. Old buildings were beaten down to rubble during the day, vanishing entirely overnight. High wooden fences sprang up, set with little windows so that curious passers-by could peer through them and watch the birth of car parks, drive-in liquor stores and office blocks. Heavy trucks drove up with huge, revolving drums on their backs, and began spewing out grey, porridgy torrents of concrete which waiting men immediately began to spread into place. Suspended above the new surfaces, which were in the process of being created, were walkways of wood, heavy planks along which men could push barrows – a maze hanging above the tender new crust of the city.

Angela and Tycho hesitated, looking through one such

fence, but Angela's mind was now on something else. She was hurrying towards her *fait accompli*.

"Where are we off to?" Tycho asked.

"You'll see," she said and then, "I won't tell you because it mightn't happen."

Past a second-hand clothes shop and a book shop, mostly paperbacks and magazines. Past a craft shop from which the smell of incense flowed as thick as treacle. Dresses of Indian cotton, cushions embroidered in coloured wools with flower petals set around little round mirrors made an unexpectedly bright glitter in the shabbiness as they hurried by. Past a shop called *Cupid's Friend*, selling remarkable red and black underwear and what it vaguely described as 'marital aids', past a shabby restaurant with a blackboard outside it promising an infinity of chips with everything, past a pub where car dealers were reputed to gather, boasting over their clever deals in car-dealer language.

"It put me back a hundred slides for the heat and beat," Tycho had once heard one man say to another, coming out of that very establishment. It had made him feel he should only come here with a passport and a translator. Yet it was only a block away from the polytechnic.

In one deep, wide doorway framed in reflecting glass so that they were accompanied by their own ghosts, a gang of young men had collected, their motorbikes, a string of iron monsters, stabled along the edge of the footpath. They wore denim jackets with the sleeves torn out, and their strong arms, bared to the city air, were tattooed with skulls, naked women and tigers being strangled by serpents. Tycho did not dare to meet the eyes of these men, some of them very little older than he was, in case they read something there at which they might take offence. Feeling furtive and cowardly, he became convinced he was approaching a tribe of *true* men, all illustrated with the signs of violence and violation, while he was an imitation creature protected by nothing but an Ionian view of the world – the belief that things might be understood, and that he might attain wonderful power at last through struggling to understand them. Angela, however, seemed to increase in self-confidence approaching the doorway, as if she knew that, during daylight hours at least, she had power over the true men, that her long legs in their tight jeans would carry her triumphantly past, desirable but unobtainable. Tycho heard their conversation stop as she walked by, there was a second or two of silence and then, from behind, a chorus of whistles and howls burst out. Tycho groaned under his breath, but to his agitation Angela stopped and turned and faced her admirers, which made the cries first hesitate, and then increase in volume. Yet there was something almost good-natured suddenly on both sides, as if by mutual acknowledgement Angela and the young men had established an understanding in common, and were prepared to be entertained by one another. All Tycho felt was the great unease of an animal in another animal's territory.

They came to a place where three roads ran into one another, and on the other side of this complicated crossover their street had changed. The transformation was completed here. From the opposite footpath a new bank building reared up – a precipice of glass, where hundreds of mirror windows reflected the buildings opposite, distorting them as they did so. At pavement level, Tycho could see a man feeding a card into a money machine which generously disgorged cash into his waiting hands. Tycho almost expected to see him click his heels and leap joyously into the air like his counterpart in a television advertisement, but he merely stumped off, stowing his money away as he went. Through the glass door pot-plants made a small, decorative jungle in the foyer. Some office girl would dust them each morning and put 'Leaf-Shine' on their leaves, but no whooping Tarzans would spring out of this tame little forest.

They now came to an elegant arcade lined with tiny shops – a dress shop, a handbag boutique, windows filled with pottery, silk-screened scarfs, prettily made artificial flowers and, facing on to the street, a coffee bar with a lot of natural stained wood in evidence and posters in the window advertising the city ballet and a play. It looked quite expensive.

"Have you got any money?" Angela hissed. Tycho searched his pocket for his wallet.

"Two dollars!" he said.

"Is that all?" she asked. "I think it's more expensive here."

"More expensive than what?" he asked, half-whispering because she had become urgent, secret and conspiratorial.

"Than across the road!" she said, and Tycho, glancing nervously across the road, saw a teashop certainly older and shabbier than the place Angela was bent on entering.

"If it's cheaper, let's go there," he suggested.

"No, I want to go here!" she said. "I think coffee costs about ninety cents a cup because it's particularly real, or black, or strong, or they make it smell as if it was."

"Or they overcharge," Tycho suggested.

Angela grinned.

"Or that!" she agreed, counting her own money.

"I'm starving, and all I've got is a dollar-fifty – well, it's better than nothing. We'll get a big slice of pizza and share it between us, but I'll have the biggest bit because I'm taller. That's symmetry."

"Selective symmetry," Tycho said, "because I'm putting more into the kitty."

Behind the clear plastic, fresh sandwiches were oozing with delicious fillings, and cakes, glazed or iced, or jewelled with coloured sugar, shone like rare treasures generously displayed. It was just before afternoon teatime. Angela was able to choose a window table and selected one at the very end of the long window where she could see, but still be partly hidden from the street outside. She took out a little mirror from her kitbag, studied her face carefully, then combed her hair so that the widow's peak was revealed clearly and the hair on either side of it sprang back in strong, red wings. She took out her dark glasses and put them on even though they were sitting in the shade.

"What's going on?" said Tycho. Angela did not reply directly.

"Don't look so guilty," she said. "It's nothing wrong!"

Tycho picked up her mirror, and looked at himself in it.

"It's not guilt," he told her. "I'm anxious. I don't know what you're up to, but I've got the feeling it's something I won't want to be mixed up in."

"Are you a man or a mouse?" Angela demanded.

"Squeak! Squeak!" said Tycho. "I've already been frightened by the thought that that tattooed gang back there might leap on you in broad daylight. I mean I'd have to make some attempt to defend you, wouldn't I, and then…" He punched his right hand into the palm of his left. "Oh well, maybe they'd have merely crippled me if they were in a good mood – I mean, being summer and the birds singing and all that; they're probably kind at heart."

"You could have run away," Angela said. "Of course," she added, "you'd never have been able to live with yourself afterwards."

"I'd have had to take to drink!" said Tycho, cheering up.

"Drowning the memory of my cries, night after night!" Angela agreed with enthusiasm.

"…my face all bleak with despair…"

"…a prey to the bitter torments of remorse," concluded Angela triumphantly.

"…or I might have joined in, I suppose," Tycho said as another possibility occurred to him. "Stood at the end of the queue."

"I don't know about you, Big Science!" Angela said, suddenly looking relaxed and entertained. "That's gross! You might amount to something after all."

"Not that I think rape's a thing to joke about," Tycho added virtuously, "but it would only make about point naught

naught two per cent of difference to you at that stage. I'd be mad not to."

"Irrational! Censored by Pythagoras!" Angela agreed. "I'd probably have fainted by then anyway."

But as they constructed this drama, he felt rather than saw her eyes flicker from his face to the street outside and back again.

She touched his arm.

"Look over there!" she said.

Tycho turned, and stared more or less where she seemed to be pointing. Across the road was a three-storey building with one big sign over the door and another running above the ground-floor windows. *Roland Chase Agencies – Filtration and Insulation, Chemicals, Photographic Equipment, Marine Accessories, Art Supplies, Electronics.*

"It's an importer's place, isn't it?" Tycho asked, not very interested. It was the sort of place you see over and over again all your life, and still never know quite where it is when someone asks you how to get to it.

"There he is," Angela said. "Crossing the road!"

"Who?" asked Tycho, staring at two men coming towards them.

"I'm involved with an older man!" Angela said. "He usually comes over here for coffee." Her fingers still lay on Tycho's arm. With her other hand she put her coffee cup into her saucer.

The two men came into the coffee bar. Tycho had never seen either of them, yet immediately he knew the taller of the two very well. In he came – well-dressed in an expensive suit (more than well-dressed – actually rather elegant), smiling a charming and familiar smile, showing even white teeth. Coppery red hair curving back in strong waves from a noticeable widow's peak pointed down on to his wide forehead, an arrowhead directing attention to other features of his handsome face. It took Tycho a long, puzzled moment to begin realising exactly what he was seeing.

That's Angela's hair, he thought stupidly. He was looking at a new version of her face, squarer than hers, being translated into masculine planes and angles, but for all that an appearance he knew by heart.

As he stared, there was the sound of a chair shifting. Angela stood up and, taking off her dark glasses, looked straight into the eyes of the taller man, certainly challenging him to speak to her, or at least notice her. In a way his reaction was satisfactory – even a little dramatic, for his mouth fell open slightly in the middle of a sentence and his eyebrows sloped in over his nose, almost as if he had winced with disapproval or pain, but then he looked bored and irritated and went on talking, rattling words out as rapidly as before, but rather more loudly as if he were drowning out another insistent voice.

"...and we just might get the agency now Honeywell's collapsed," he was saying. "I wouldn't mind getting into laboratory chemicals. It fits in with some of our other lines. Sit over there by the window," he directed his companion, "and you'll be able to watch the world go by – potential customers, everyone."

He had an enormously cultured accent that vaguely

suggested art and sensitivity. Sitting down, he made sure he had his back placed squarely towards them.

Angela also sat down slowly. Tycho understood she was suffering from confusion and disappointment. Her lower lip quivered a little but only because she was stiffening it against collapse. But what had she hoped for, Tycho wondered.

"I don't see why they run on so much about stiff upper lips," he said quickly. "It's bottom ones that give way."

"Don't they just!" Angela agreed, her voice quavering very slightly. She had not taken her eyes off the back of the charcoal-grey suit. "Mind you, I can see it would be difficult for him to recognise – no, he *did* recognise me, didn't he... I mean, to acknowledge me."

"Who is he?" Tycho asked in a resigned voice.

Angela looked over at him.

"Doesn't he remind you of someone?"

"Do you know his name?" Tycho persisted, looking more anxious than ever.

"He's Roland William Cheever Chase – the actual owner of that building over there," Angela said, and then suddenly made up her mind to tell all of a secret that was virtually told anyway. "I'm about ninety-nine per cent sure he's my father." And it seemed to Tycho that, just for a moment, he actually felt the wobble in the heart of the world as a great hesitation in the solid existence of chairs and tables, and men and women too. Angela looked eagerly into his face from across the table, and Tycho felt himself grow prophetic and cold, as if the hesitation had stolen warmth out of his very heart.

6

ON BEING A CHILD OF LOVE

"Ninety-nine per cent sure!" Tycho repeated after her, after pretending to calculate and gaining a little time. "That's a pretty high probability – almost dead certain." He stared at Angela, then turned to the wide, grey back across the coffee bar. "How did you find him? Just see him in the street one day?"

Angela leaned across the table.

"Before we came to Dry Creek Road," she said, "we used to live in a little room – a sort of shed really – at the back of an old man's house. Dido was a cross between a nurse and a housekeeper for him. Every evening she used to read to us, but then, last thing, she'd tell me a special secret story called *The Great Chase* and it was all about a wonderful girl called Angela Roland. Maybe the story carried on into Dry Creek Road time for a bit. I don't know. I'm pretty sure it had stopped by the time I went to school. It puts our names together though – Angela and Roland, I mean."

"Not much to go on," Tycho said.

"Give me a chance!" Angela muttered. "I'm trying to make it orderly for you. You see, for ages I didn't much worry about not having a father. Lots of people are missing one parent or the other and I was just one of the broken-home gang." She lifted her coffee cup again. "My hand's shaking," she exclaimed in surprise. "Blast! I hate feeling so – so affected by things."

She put the cup down and waved her hand across the table at Tycho.

"There they go," she said. "All my pretty little trembles!" and Tycho imagined them flying away through the coffee bar, transparent trembles, carried away on glassy wings.

"It was just as if he was dead – unobtainable anyway," Angela went on. "And he wasn't real – just a poetical idea – the great love of Dido's life, and she could never love anyone else afterwards. Other people's mothers and fathers played around a bit, but Dido was always true."

"Right on!" exclaimed Tycho clapping his hands together. Angela frowned at him.

"Sometimes I used to get a crush on some other girl's father – or feel slightly jealous! Nothing very heavy though." She shot a glance across the room, which was filling up as afternoon teatime began to dominate the city. "And then one day I suddenly woke up to the fact that he wasn't dead and he wasn't just a poetical idea. He was actually here in the same city as me. I could see him, I could talk to him. But when I asked, Dido clammed up on me and wouldn't say a word. It's gone on like that for quite a while now. I've pestered, and she's stalled. Not all at once, of course. It's been little by little, and a whole lot of cat-and-mousing around, but it *is* natural to want to know, isn't it?"

Tycho thought it was utterly natural, but the thought only

filled him with increasing alarm, for no one knew better than he did how strong natural feelings could be, and also how wrong it was to believe that natural things, given in to, would automatically bring happiness. He began drawing invisible lines on the table with the handle of his teaspoon. The pizza lay between them, Angela's slice only half-eaten and his own, smaller piece untouched.

"So?" he prompted her.

"Well, I got so fed up with not knowing, that a little while ago I pinched Dido's key and went through her file one evening when she was out. She has this metal filing cabinet with our birth certificates and mortgage payments and so on in it. I thought she might have love letters or something."

"Would you have read them – someone else's letters?" Tycho asked, and Angela gave him a mulish look.

"Yes," she said. "Well, maybe not all through, unless they were really interesting – just enough to find out his name. Anyhow I didn't have to. There weren't any love letters, but there was a different, official-looking letter addressed to Roland Chase, something Dido had written ages ago, going by the envelope. It was all wilted and ratty, and it was addressed care of a lawyer, no other address, but once I saw the name, all that old story came rushing back to me. I'd forgotten about it for years, but suddenly there it was: *The Great Chase* – starring Angela Roland. Dido's like you and me – she plays word games – makes jokes and puns – she'd play a game automatically without working it out properly." Saying this Angela picked up her own teaspoon and began stirring her coffee, although she took no sugar, frowning down into the heart of the spiral made by the stirring spoon.

"It makes the same pattern as a galaxy," commented Tycho, also staring at the spiral. "There's something called the doctrine of signatures that sees a great universal relationship between similar patterns that seem accidental to the rest of us."

"What's that got to do with anything?" Angela asked sharply.

"I don't know. Nothing, I suppose," Tycho said humbly. "I was just mentioning it. I promise I wasn't trying to change the subject."

"I was just remembering something," Angela said. "Nothing to tell about." She had been remembering waking up in the night many, many years earlier, and hearing a sound that had puzzled her. It had been before she and Dido had moved to Dry Creek Road, and she had been sleeping then in a funny old cot. The slats of its sides rose up out of the past like the bars of a cage and she remembered lying very still because sometimes forceful movements made the bottom fall out of it. There, from that wooden cage, long since chopped up for firewood, she had heard, for the first time, a sound as small and private as the murmur of the creek earlier in the afternoon, the sound of lonely crying – Dido crying in the dark.

"It was pretty easy after that, really," she said to Tycho. "I just looked him up in the phone book first of all, and there he was – his address in this street and another one, 67a Rosegarden Drive."

"Smart address," Tycho said, putting on an expression of exaggerated respect.

"It's an enormous house." Angela looked both eager and resentful. "I've seen it. Tennis court, swimming pool, the lot."

"How long ago was this?" Tycho asked. "I mean how long since you…"

"Not very long. The first expedition was just after the maths exam," she told him. "It was a morning exam and I shot off afterwards."

Catching a bus, she had sat with a map on her knee, checking off names from street corners. At last she had got off the bus, had walked across a pretty park to find herself among big, old houses on big, old properties, all silently saying one word over and over again: "money, money, money". At last there it was – a white house at the top of a green lawn – a ship upraised on a wave of well-tended grass, dormer windows and a pillared verandah, old, established trees and a drive in the form of a big semicircle with a new car parked outside the panelled door. A red retriever had lain on the step staring over at her with sad nobility.

She noticed Tycho begin to scratch a small scar on the knuckle of one thumb with the nail of the other. He had begun to look vague in a way that meant he was troubled. In moments of stress he often looked as if he were trying not to exist. "Any kids?" he asked.

"I didn't see any, but there are at least three older than I am," Angela said. "I mean that was the point of the whole great, noble sacrifice." Her voice was filled with both respect and resentment. "But that was his arrangement with Dido. Neither of them made any arrangement with me, did they? I almost walked up then and there, and knocked at the door, but I chickened out. Anyway he would have been at work – over there." She jerked her head at the sign across the road. "Sorting and importing!"

"Wobbling!" Tycho murmured, but if Angela heard this she gave no sign.

"I came here next," she recalled, wrinkling her forehead as if she were remembering something that happened years ago. "In that tearoom across the road there's a place you can sit and see right *down* the street, and there's a long mirror on the wall that shows you what's coming *up* it towards you. It was good fun, like being a spy. But I didn't really know what I was looking for." Angela paused, and directed a glance at the man at the opposite end of the window. Other people now sat between them, but as cars passed in the street beyond, distorted reflections of his face swam in and out of existence on the surface of the glass. "Well, I *did* know in a way," she admitted. "I knew he had red hair like mine. Dido once told me that, ages ago in the days when she wanted to talk about him, just as if it was something he'd specially arranged. And I know he's paid us money. Dido says he's let us have what he could afford without setting his own family back." Angela frowned. "It can't have been much, because we've always been so poor. That crazy house we live in – it's just as well I like it, because we can only afford something no one else wants. We always have to have enough in the bank each month to cover the mortgage payments. It bugged me to see that great white whale of a house and the huge lawn. I suppose I've got slightly obsessed by now. I can't put it out of my head."

Tycho spoke at last. "I wouldn't say he was thrilled to see you," he said bluntly.

"No – well, he wouldn't be, would he? Not in public," Angela agreed, but rather as if she were sticking up for the man.

"Is this the first time you've stood in front of him like that?" Tycho asked.

"Yes," said Angela, "but it's not the first time he's seen me. The very first time I came here – Bingo! – I saw him crossing the road... just as easy as that. I was in the tearoom over there, and he walked across the road to this place with a really swept-up girl not much older than me – my half-sister, I suppose."

Tycho looked dubious. Angela stared around the coffee bar, apparently searching it for clues to the mystery of her own existence.

"You see, at first I thought just me *seeing* him would be enough, but then I got so I wanted *him* to see *me*. I wanted him to stand still and look at me properly. That's natural, isn't it?" she asked as she had asked once already. Tycho arched his pale eyebrows, opened his mouth and shut it again.

"Fair enough?" persisted Angela, thumping the table slightly.

"Fair..." said Tycho. "Fair but..."

"Your old symmetry again! You think it's wrong to depend on it," Angela exclaimed. Tycho nodded and grimaced.

"But I've got to try. If you worried too much about being disappointed you'd never do anything," she said, and raised her voice slightly. "It's not as if I want to *bother* anyone. I don't want to get more money, or even take up any time. I just want to say 'Hello' and to know who he is." Her voice dropped again. "And I suppose I want him to know who I am and feel sorry at what he's missed out on. Reasonable?"

"Yes, but what's the use of being reasonable when no one else is!" Tycho said. "It doesn't seem to me he's been reasonable himself, not ever seeing you or taking an interest."

"I told you, he was married with three kids – possibly more by now," Angela pointed out. "See, that's why games like old-friends and romantic-notions mean something to me. Dido and Roland had to part, but they planned to be united for ever in their baby. Nothing would ever take them apart again. They would be married in every cell in me – biology and mystery. Your kind of stuff. Chromosomes and DNA. My kind of stuff too, I suppose."

"Did Dido tell you that?" Tycho asked, fascinated. "Or did you make it up afterwards?" He could certainly imagine having that sort of thought himself.

"She used to tell me things like that," Angela said. "When we did chromosomes in biology I already knew all about them. They were a lover's knot. But I used to be more than what I am now. I used to be your actually guaranteed true love." Then she dropped her flippant tone and said with passion, "I *was* true love, so no wonder I can't help being curious about it all. I'll never know who I am – no, not that..." She stopped and then muttered, "I'll just never know unless..." and stopped again. "You see, being illegitimate..."

"That doesn't matter nowadays," Tycho said quickly.

Angela's eyes grew rounder and hotter with indignation at his interruption.

"Oh, doesn't it?" she said. "And I suppose it didn't matter to anyone when your father got hurt, and people started making snide remarks about him?"

"People don't care whether other people's parents are married or not. They don't feel threatened by that," Tycho argued, astonished that there could be any question.

"No one cares *much*," Angela corrected him. "Much! But it's like living at a poor address – it marks you off, and every now and then, when people ask you, it's as if you always have to give them too much information about yourself. They label you, and the label's like a weight."

Tycho thought there was a lot of labelling in the world, and that it was impossible to escape it.

"Everyone labels," he said. "We all do. It's convenient. Brand names are labels, and you follow brand names." Beyond them three women sat down at a table, and Roland Chase and his companion became entirely invisible except for the steady flicker on the window.

"I always felt worth more than most of you," Angela said. "Well, more in some ways and not so much in others. I was truly *meant*, even though Dido wanted me to be a boy. Truly *meant*! Dido said when she first saw me she knew at once that it had been me all the time. She said I was kicking and red – face and hair both – and very cross at being born, and very mysterious."

Angela's face was flooded with tenderness, as if it were a love affair of her own she was describing. "If ever I have a baby, that's what I'm going to feel for it," she promised fervently, and Tycho was filled with panic because he thought he was actually going to shed tears. He set his teeth, opened his eyes rather wider and stared blankly into the air, hoping his eyes would drink back their own salt water rather than insist on trickling it down on either side of his sunburnt nose. Angela laughed, slightly self-consciously.

"They loved each other madly, passionately!" she said smiling, inviting Tycho to smile too, though what she really wanted was his sympathy not his amusement.

"I can remember Africa saying that that was how she loved Hudson," he remarked. "She yelled at my parents, 'But I love Hudson! I can't live without him!' and threw her cup on the floor. You could hear her all over the house."

The two men stood up. They had talked as incessantly as Angela and Tycho, had had two cups of coffee each and were now leaving the coffee bar. Roland Chase moved carefully between the crowded tables, crabbing slightly to prevent any part of his face turning to their corner of the room.

"I passed him in the street a few times," Angela told Tycho, her eyes flicking at Roland Chase's back until it seemed he must feel her gaze, like a hand, tapping on his shoulder. But he neither hesitated, turned or stopped chatting to his companion. "First I watched him from the tearoom over there, and then last week I started to move out and cross the street at the same time as he was coming back from here. Well, I don't think he noticed me much the first two times, but the day before yesterday I wore my old shorts..."

"I remember," Tycho nodded. "Go on!"

"Well, he certainly noticed me then," Angela said with satisfaction. "And after we'd passed each other, we both turned round and looked back at each other."

Outside, the two men, seeing a gap in the traffic, launched themselves briskly over the street.

"Well, he might be your old man," Tycho said, "but if I was you I'd write him off. I think he's a bit of a creep."

"You think any good-looking man has to be a bit of a creep," argued Angela. "Being plain is making you twisted."

"I don't mind a bit of a twist," Tycho replied casually, not bothering to deny it. "A right-handed helical twist like honeysuckle."

"Ha ha! Very funny," Angela said. "Nothing as sweet and natural as that, I'm afraid, my dear."

"You go on about nature," Tycho said, "as if it was just simple. But it's natural for people to be unnatural in some ways. We're nature red in tooth and claw, *and* nature read in truth and law, both at the same time. Anyhow I think we'd better move on too. It's the sort of place where they expect you to keep on eating and drinking or get out, and we've been here ages."

"Hang on while I finish my piece of pizza," Angela said. "We've paid for it..." A moment later she said rather wistfully, "You're not eating yours."

"You have it," Tycho said. "I don't want it."

"You're a really fussy eater," Angela said, wrapping the remaining slice in a paper napkin. "I'll take it home in my kitbag, and anyhow – did you make that up what you just said a moment ago?"

"What was that?" Tycho asked.

"About nature read in truth and law!"

"I did make it up, but not exactly on the spur of the moment," Tycho admitted. "I thought of it once during an exam, but I couldn't think of any good way of working it in at the time so I saved it up. It just suddenly came in useful."

"Terrific, Big Science!" Angela said. "It's just as well you're so short – it's a sort of justice. Nature read in truth and law – it's an opposite, isn't it? What we're supposed to end up by being like – civilised and all that."

"The thing is, what are you going to do about you-know-what?" Tycho asked as they came out on to the street again.

"I don't know! Nothing probably," Angela said. However, they both knew she was lying. It was not in her nature to do nothing. "Don't tell anyone, will you?" she added hastily.

"What do you take me for?" Tycho demanded indignantly. "But why don't you tell Dido and stop playing ghosts out of the past. Dangerous meetings in the middle of the road, traffic whizzing by."

"Romantic encounters," Angela corrected him. "I might turn out to be the daughter he's always longed for."

"It didn't look like it," Tycho said. "Don't begin dreaming of it."

They drove back to Tycho's house, rather on edge with each other, and met his mother in the drive, just back from her china-painting class. She had brought her latest work of art home – a white china teapot painted with apples and blackberry blossom, and now proposed to christen the pot immediately by making tea in it. Angela praised the painting. Tycho could see that though its old-fashioned prettiness was not the sort of thing she usually admired, she was really impressed by it because it had been painted by someone she actually knew whose skill showed. They were neither hungry nor thirsty, but tea in a new teapot painted with apples and blackberry blossom had a charm about it they could not resist. They watched the amber tea leap from the spout and both thought briefly of the little golden pools they had looked into earlier in the afternoon.

"I do hope you remembered to get something for Africa's anniversary," Mrs Potter said to Tycho.

"I'll get it tomorrow," Tycho said. "It won't be much. I'm broke."

"I'll give you something towards it," Mrs Potter said hastily. "It's for a good cause."

She was so pleased with her teapot (and grateful for the praise Angela had lavished on it) that she was particularly gracious to Angela, almost losing the reserve she usually showed towards her. A strange, temporary peace settled over the three of them until Dido arrived in her car. She tooted for Angela, who thanked Mrs Potter for having her and for the cup of tea, and went out promising to see Tycho in the morning.

7

A ROAD OF BLOOD
AND FLOWERS

There were no blinds on Angela's window and she did not bother to pull the skimpy curtains. But though she often woke with the first light, she seldom got up until the very last moment. This solitary time was precious, a time for bringing everything together, lining up yesterday with the day ahead. Beginning such a day she might think of Robin and the band they had heard the previous night, or of Tycho matching up a lack of symmetry in the heart of matter with a lack of fairness in everyday life, or the two memories might run together, all the more interesting for being mixed. However, on this particular morning she woke with the feeling that there was still an exam in front of her, one she had put in long hours working for, taking pages and pages of notes and, just for a moment, she lay, eyes shut, frowning and trying to remember exactly which exam it might be. The room was crossed with slanting blades of early sunlight. She was like a magician's lady shut in a box pierced through with golden swords. But she herself was impenetrable, able, once the swords were withdrawn, to rise up, triumphant and whole. Crossing her arms on her breast, putting her hands on their opposite shoulders, she hugged herself drowsily, imagining herself not a girl so much as a shimmering bird flying unharmed through a country of archers. After a moment such fairy-tale thoughts as these gave way to the realisation that what was ahead of her was not an exam, but the moment when she and her father would call each other by name at last.

She opened her eyes, turned on to her back and stared at the ceiling. There was a crack directly overhead. Many years ago when they had first come to 1000 Dry Creek Road with their few possessions – a bed settee, saucepans, sheets and blankets – the crack had been there waiting for her. She had named it, "Mr Dead's Smile". Mr Dead had been a ghost who came down when the lights were turned off so that he could gobble her up, but Angela had never been afraid of Mr Dead, only thrilled by him, for she always knew she was much cleverer than he was. In her pillow stories she killed him, night after night, and stole his smile. Sometimes, for a change, he would fall in love with her and give it up freely, but he had never got the better of her, not even in dreams, and a girl who could command Mr Dead would command a father with no trouble at all. Her plan was simply to give up waiting for Roland Chase to speak to her in the public streets and coffee bars, to go to his office, call him by his name and give him hers so that he must speak to her.

Having decided what her plan must be, she tried it out with various endings. Some made her smile, some made her scornful. Muttering pieces of dialogue aloud, she anticipated questions and invented answers for them, but as she invented, she smiled less and less. Her eyes began to fill with tears and the tears flowed slowly down her cheeks, though not because of any straightforward sadness. As they trickled past her mouth she intercepted them by putting out her tongue, tasting her own salt. She was puzzled by these drops squeezed out of her by feelings which, pulling in opposite directions, wrung her so that somewhere deep inside a subterranean ocean was worked on and made to creep out through her eyes. However, Angela had always suspected an oddity in her geography and knew, because she had access to this ocean, that in a funny way she was bigger inside than out. She took a note of this idea as something to pass on to Tycho, who had once demonstrated the strange behaviour of the Mobius strip to her – two sides and a single surface. It seemed a similar idea.

There were footsteps on the verandah.

"Angela," called Dido. "Get up early. Let's have a picnic breakfast."

Usually breakfast was the sort of meal gone before it had really begun. They rushed to and fro, a slice of toast in one hand, an iron in the other. "I'm ironing *crumbs* into my skirt," Dido had wailed only last week. Early morning was a time for arguments and recrimination and blaming each other, not only for things that were going wrong in that particular hour, but for things that had gone wrong last week and last year, a time for pointing out faults in one another's characters. Morning was a time when, baying from one room to another, they demanded instant apology and promises to reform. However, this morning it was to be different – it was a picnic breakfast, a treat Dido sometimes arranged unexpectedly.

And why this morning, Angela wondered uneasily, if Dido hadn't somehow pulled her intentions out of the air, and wondered too whether she was about to be confronted with arguments and prohibitions? But there was nothing threatening. Dido had pulled the cane table out on to the verandah, covered it with a white cloth embroidered sixty years earlier by her godmother, and set it with a jug of apple and orange juice, muesli and milk. The toaster sat self-consciously on an apple box, trailing a long tail behind it – the extension cord usually used on the rare occasions when they vacuumed the car. It coiled on the worn planking, and snaked in through the open window, attaching itself to the plug on the stove like an electric lamprey. Dido, dressed in a blue dress and sandals, had brushed her hair and tied it back with a blue scarf. She looked worn, Angela thought, but as if she still had a lot of wear in her, being both soft and tough – soft leather spread over a skeleton of wire and springy steel. Smiling, she made deep creases like brackets in her cheeks, and Angela found herself considering the possibility that smiles were not an essential part of Dido's life, even though she smiled so often, but merely cheerful interruptions (always appearing in parenthesis). And yet, in their life together, smiles, like breakfast picnics, had always seemed to be part of the essence.

"What on earth time did you get in last night?" Dido

asked casually. It sounded like a leading question, but she had a book on the table and, as she spoke, her eyes slid sideways to it, while her voice grew slightly absent-minded.

"One o'clock," Angela replied.

The toaster twanged and two pieces of lightly-browned toast leapt buoyantly into the air.

"And the rest!" Dido said derisively. "I was up until one myself. Where did you go?"

"The Gladstone," said Angela, who always told the truth now that she felt she was old enough to get away with it. "There was a group we wanted to hear. And then I went to the Victoria Coffee Club with Robin and some other people." She left it at that. Such descriptions of the evening were usually enough. Dido tapped at the cover of her book. Angela almost expected to see it open of its own accord and line after line of words march out like soldiers parading before a general.

"Was it good?" she asked. "The band, I mean."

"Too much heavy guitar," Angela said, subduing her toast with butter and lime marmalade. "It's not a big space."

"They're always too loud," Dido said, "or they sound too loud to me."

"No, they're meant to be loud," Angela assured her. "It's a way of being overwhelmed. It's exciting, like a great test."

"But not of intelligence, only stamina," Dido replied. "Isn't it a terrific morning?" Saying this she opened her book. "We've got about twenty minutes," she added. The morning was beautiful. Angela could not see a single cloud in the sky. The tops of the trees further down the slope made a soft green fringe of spiky lace against the blue. Angela, who knew breakfast picnics of old, opened her own book.

"I hope you didn't drink too much!" Dido suddenly said, without looking up from her first page.

Since she hadn't even begun her own first page, Angela was free to frown reprovingly at her mother.

"Here, did you set up a breakfast picnic just to *inquisit* me," she cried indignantly. "What a – a *motherly* thing to do," she added bitterly.

Dido merely laughed, half-penitently.

"I didn't mean to inquisit – but I do worry. First I worry about you, because the road is very greasy at the present and I just get the feeling it's – it's looking for someone... that it wants blood. You know that feeling I get."

Angela did indeed know. It filled her with anxiety, partly because it was evidence of Dido's craziness that she should believe the road was strangely alive and requiring a victim, but more because she immediately believed it too. Dido, partly mythological herself, was the sort of person who might recognise a mythological road.

"I know the road like the back of my hand!" Angela cried, which was true. "I've been up and down that road twice a day most days for years and years – it sits up and begs if I want it to."

"And then even if *you* get by all right, I worry about the car," Dido added. "I mean it's not very reliable, and it's not insured."

"Insure it!" Angela cried. "Go on – while it's still got a warrant!"

"I will," Dido said, beginning to read again. However, by now Angela had become interested in the car and its quality of life, and was reminded of a deeper issue.

"You won't," she said challengingly, "and it's not because you couldn't afford to have it fixed up if there was anything wrong with it. It's just that in a way you enjoy things being inefficient."

"I do not!" exclaimed Dido, indignant in turn.

"You do so!" Angela replied. "Look at the house. You could afford to have a door knocked between the bedrooms and the living room now. It's a real pain to have to walk out on to the verandah to go from one room to another, particularly in the winter. And why don't we have a septic tank put in? We could afford it now, and it'll be a million years before they bring sewerage this far up the hill."

"I'm so used to it, I forget it can be changed," Dido said apologetically.

"You grapple disadvantages to you with hoops of steel!" said Angela. Two more pieces of toast leapt, like two-dimensional creatures. "Tycho says that maybe you've spent so much time and energy struggling with our disadvantages that now they've grown to be part of you and you won't change them."

Dido topped up her glass of fruit juice.

"I wonder... It might be half true," she said slowly and added, "Why don't you go out with Tycho? Then I wouldn't live in dread of the phone going at one-thirty in the morning, and the police telling me you've been caught drinking in a pub underage, or that they're just taking you out of the wreckage of a car and what do I want done with the pieces."

"I could get wiped out by his fatalistic ideas though," Angela said. "He can be really funny, but he's not light-hearted. It's not his fault that he isn't, but I love light-heartedness."

Yet at the same time she remembered Tycho standing in the little gully shouting at her about symmetry, or talking later in the day about her father and saying, "If I were you, I think I'd write him off," demonstrating his own brand of ruthlessness.

"I like it better when we're on our own – Tyke and me," Angela said. "He comes up with funny things... I want to pull his leg about them at the time – and then I find I go on thinking about them – they stick in my thoughts. I really *love* Tyke as a friend – better than almost anyone else. Actually, once or twice..." She stopped and shot a glance at Dido who was listening, but still reading in a sideways fashion. "I've given him a few chances," Angela confessed. "'Here I am! Take me!' I've said (not those actual words of course). But he's too screwed-up about himself, let alone me. It's always turned out too embarrassing to be worthwhile."

Dido nodded without looking up.

Angela was not quite sure she hadn't been talking to herself. "Were you listening?" she asked.

"Of course!" Dido replied. "I always listen, even if it doesn't always show."

After they had prepared for the day they packed themselves into the old Triumph Herald, Angela in tight blue jeans, a thin, fine shirt made rather more modest because she was wearing a plum-coloured T-shirt over it. Sometimes she liked the contrast between this rich colour and her hair, and then sometimes she thought it looked dreadful, and because she couldn't be sure, the T-shirt was almost new. Unexpectedly she flung her arm over Dido's shoulder and gave her a kiss on the cheek.

"What was that for?" asked Dido, looking pleased, but a little doubtful.

"Because!" cried Angela triumphantly. "Just because. And also you need to be reminded. Too much solitude isn't good for you."

"Solitude!" Dido began searching for the car key. "I'm with people at work all day. And anyhow you should be glad I like solitude. It sets both of us free – you too."

"Yes, but you've given up giving me good advice," Angela cried. "Why don't you forbid me to go to pubs and things? That's what a responsible mother would do. You used to advise me."

Dido looked surprised and then concerned, automatically turning the car key so that the car sprang to life, shuddering, as if reluctant to begin the journey ahead. "But you *hated* the advice!" she said. "We had such dreadful fights. And you say you want to hear these bands, and there's nowhere else you can go to hear them, not unless you go to those big concerts and they're just so expensive."

"Anyhow we're interested in the local groups and not the big time commercial stuff," Angela said rather grandly. "You don't have to worry. We don't have enough money to drink much, and anyhow Robin's always training for something."

Dido released the handbrake and the car began its descent, a slow, courtly roll towards the first corner.

"Besides," said Dido, "as far as I can see I have a very strange choice. Either I let you go and worry about you, which I do, or I can keep you home and have you raging around complaining about me, the place we live in, and probably in the end telling me a few lies about where you're going and who you're going out with and so on."

"A lot of kids have to do that," Angela agreed almost virtuously.

The car dipped down a slope and she added, looking at the rocks and the wild slope beginning on either side of them, "Isn't it funny? Every day we go from tooth and claw to truth and law and back again... you and me together." She was talking about the road, suddenly thrilled to think everyday life had given her such clear signs to follow.

Up here at its conclusion Dry Creek Road whipped backwards and forwards in a series of hairpin bends. At certain points, these bends looked out into space. There seemed to be nothing at all in front of them or even under the wheels of the car but pure air, though from further down the hill, looking up and back, it was possible to see they were actually underpinned by slopes, sharp but substantial, streaked at this time of the year with the bright yellow of flowering gorse and broom, and rank on rank of foxgloves, purple, pink and white, rising high and tall out of the thin grass, their tops bent under the weight of their own buds, gazing down on the slopes below them.

"A lot of kids lie to their parents," Angela said. "A lot of parents don't have the faintest idea what's going on."

"It's not fair though!" Dido replied, frowning. "People want to trust their children, and they want them safe. Who wants death or tears?"

"But being strict doesn't stop things like that," Angela said cheerfully.

"It might lessen the chances of them," Dido replied. "I just don't always know."

Across space they could see other hillsides of sheep-nibbled green. They were now separated from the abyss by the worst fences in the world. Stock often wandered up through gaps out on to the road and they had to drive carefully, just in case. Today a sheep, recently shorn, lean and goatish in its basic skin, ran ahead of them with a large, fat, woolly lamb, undocked, running beside it, its long tail bumping wildly up and down. Mother and child found a gap and vanished in a little scatter of stones and a cloud of dust.

Around the next bend they came upon Dry Creek Bridge straddling the flow of barren stones. A car, almost the duplicate of their own, was parked there, and two young men armoured like space men were setting off to spray gorse, cylinders on their backs, masked against fumes, the nozzles of the sprays moving in front of them like Geiger counters.

"Phil and Jerry Cherry!" exclaimed Angela with hatred.

"Now then, Angela – don't go making any coarse signs," Dido cried. "I just hate that sort of thing to begin with, and then they are neighbours."

"Some neighbours!" Angela said furiously. "They shot Tonbridge." Tonbridge had been their cat.

"We don't know that it was them," Dido said rather feebly.

"We do!" cried Angela. "It's a high probability. You're just scared of them."

"I am a bit," Dido admitted. "We're a long way away from anyone up there, and I just get the feeling that they're the sort of boys who might get a skinful in, and then think it would be funny to slaughter a sheep on our verandah or throw stones at our windows or God knows what!"

"I'm not going to be subtle with them. They give us the fingers!" Angela declared. "Ignoring them is sort of defeatist, like giving in to the forces of evil. They won't go away."

"I don't expect the forces of evil to go away, I just don't want to attract their attention," Dido told her. "It's bad enough when the Cherrys drive by us and lean on the horn. They really frighten me."

Deep down, however, Angela felt sure she was more than a match for the Cherry brothers.

The hillside began to flatten out. The road grew less steep. The dreadful submissions of gravity which had escorted them down over the bridge and the sharp bend beyond it grew less urgent.

"There's a new death!" Dido said suddenly. A possum lay dead on the road, crimson streaks beside it.

Every now and then Angela saw Dido noticing these random corpses with narrowed eyes, aware of her face growing sterner as if she read of an imminent attack on herself in such bloody signs. She noticed the possum in this way now.

"What's wrong?" Angela asked.

"Nothing!" said Dido. "Look, the bulldozer's out, dozing around." The road was under constant readjustment. The crumbling outer edge of one corner had recently begun to give way, and now a bulldozer was biting into the cliff on the other side, widening the road inward. Dust from oxidised volcanic rock spread a rusty blush around the whole bend. They slowed down for the lumbering bulldozer, the car engine cut out and they waited a moment while the iron beast, devouring rocks, shifted its bulk to let them by.

Road works announced a notice on the side of the road.

"So it does!" agreed Dido, and Angela heard with apprehension an odd sardonic note in Dido's voice, as though she detected another sign.

Angela, who particularly wanted Dido to be calm and mild today, just in case she didn't feel very calm and mild herself later on, was disturbed to see evidence of a darkening mood. But then suppose – just faintly suppose – she was driven home in a wonderful car, and walked in at the door and said, "Mother!" (Not that she ever called Dido "Mother", only "Dido", and occasionally "Mum".) She would turn pale, her hand would fly to her mouth. She would be torn by conflicting emotions, pride concealing her inner turmoil.

Angela described the scene to herself, her eyes unconsciously growing round, her lips parting with anticipated emotion – but Roland Chase would step forward, humble and tender, and suddenly Dido would fall into his arms. They would never be parted again. Angela laughed aloud, but this romantic idea did not melt away altogether under her determined ridicule. It was stubborn to its core and refused to budge.

"It works all the time," Dido said, referring to the road. "But it certainly needs a sacrifice or two."

"Superstition!" cried Angela.

"Maybe," Dido agreed. "But we've used this road so much it sometimes seems we might have to pay for it. It seems more like a powerful force than a mere road. Remember coming up here in the past, pushing a pram full of firewood?"

"Why were we always so poor if *he* paid us money?" Angela asked.

"He didn't pay much – just what he could afford," Dido said, "and there weren't any government benefits in those days, not after you were three months old, anyhow. It took ages and ages just to go to the shops then, let alone the school." (Dido had had a cleaning job at the school.) "Down was all right, but up... well I used to keep the pram under the bridge and carry the wood and cones up the last part. And then at last we did get a car."

"I remember it!" Angela said. "Wasn't it terrific? And then you got work and our troubles vanished."

"I wouldn't say that. New troubles began!" Dido said. They drove off the rutted shingle and on to the smooth asphalt. The car sang a little more contentedly; they actually began to glide. "But of course they were a better class of troubles than our old ones. We've never had to worry about buying food in quite the same way. Anyhow, somehow the road seems like an old friend, but that's part of its treachery... it's always likely to present a bill for services rendered."

"It's just not like you to be superstitious," Angela exclaimed.

"I'm not – well, not really," Dido said. "Every now and then I find myself feeling someone like me might have to pay a tribute. Do you want me to drop you off at Tycho's today?"

"Oh, yes – we're doing a noble anti-litter thing in the park today – a crusade against soft-drink cans and ice-cream wrappers and other infidels," Angela said. "And Tycho's allowed his mother's car to drive there, so he might as well take me too."

Houses now rushed past on either side of them. Some of them Angela had seen go up, others she had been acquainted with for fourteen years at least. She returned to her plan. Originally it had sat rough and formless in her mind – had possibly sat there unrecognised for many years. But now it was brilliant and jewel-like, wonderfully defined as it had never been before. They drove off Dry Creek Road into Centaurus Road – the road of the Centaur – and headed for Tycho's house.

8

EVENTS ARE THE
STUFF OF THE WORLD

"I think you're mad," Tycho said. "Forget it! It's a romantic notion and you're not meant to take them undiluted. Water it down! Talk about books."

But Angela went on to talk about exactly the same thing that she had been talking about before.

"Just tell me!" she demanded. "Will you wait for me here or across the road?"

"Suppose he's not there," Tycho argued, "or he doesn't want to see you?"

"Then I'll just kick his door in and come out again," Angela replied in a perfectly reasonable voice.

"I just don't think it's a good idea," Tycho repeated desperately. But as he spoke he was double-parking the car outside Roland Chase Agencies – a building which now stood out in the familiar street with troublesome significance, like Castle Perilous. His own life had become involved in it, for whatever happened to Angela beyond its doors would virtually happen to him too.

Angela twisted around and faced him.

"Why are you so sure he'll mind?" she demanded. "Don't you think I'm up to standard?"

"It's nothing to do with that," Tycho said feebly.

"Why should he mind?" Angela asked. "I'm acceptable. I won't be any trouble. I just want to hear him say my name."

Tycho looked across at her, and tried to imagine what he would feel like if a wonderful creature like Angela turned up at his door and told him he was her father. She had combed her hair so that the widow's peak was clear and visible. With her eyes round with excitement and fear, her lips folded together to hold back impetuous words, Tycho thought she looked explosive – as if she might actually burst into flames at any moment and burn furiously in the car beside him. He imagined himself scrambling desperately out of range and hearing it explode behind him.

"You *don't* just want that," he argued. "At first you *just* wanted to see him, then you *just* wanted him to see you, now you *just* want him to speak to you. Probably you'll end up by *just* wanting him to leave his family and marry Dido, and start doing what fathers do – forbidding you to go out with the wrong sort of boys, and all that stuff."

"He'd have to be understanding about that," Angela said. "I'm too set in my ways. Tyke – I don't feel I have any choice."

"You could choose not to," suggested Tycho.

Angela thought for a moment. "I couldn't," she declared sombrely at last. "I could only *pretend* to choose not to. I could easily go home with you right now, but deep down I know that I'd just sneak back tomorrow, only without telling anyone – even you – this time."

Tycho knew this was true. He admitted to himself that he might well have done the same thing if he was the child of confident passion and not of resignation. Somewhere behind them a car tooted impatiently.

"That's OK. It's not a cop," Angela said, glancing back over her shoulder. "I know it's bound to be awkward at first. I'm psyched up for that. But he has paid for me all these years. He ought to have a chance to get some return on his investment."

"OK, I'll wait," Tycho said, "but under protest."

"See you then!" Angela said hastily, and scrambled out of the car. Tycho watched her with foreboding as she walked along the footpath and in under the sign that said *Roland Chase Agencies.*

At last he drove on, going around the block twice in case she had had to come straight out again. There was no sign of her, and he found a parking place opposite a telephone box and next to a used car lot. He looked uneasily down the road and took a book from the back seat of the car – without any great enthusiasm, however. His pursuit of information about the Ionian scientists had led him to try a fat, brown book, *A History of Western Philosophy*. Here he encountered again the familiar names that touched his curiosity – Democritus, Anaxagoras, Aristarchus of Samos, Parmenides who said nothing ever moved, and Heraclitus who said everything moved the whole time, that there was no such thing as a moment's rest. All the same Tycho was not sure if he would ever be interested in this book which seemed very difficult reading, juggling with small words and narrow shades of meaning. As his eyes skimmed the pages, he was aware that powerful riddles were being asked and revealed, which might be rich in amazement. He did not really want to go on reading the book, but he did not entirely want to give it up, either. Though it was impossible to concentrate on it, there on the edge of Angela's adventure, it still distracted him in a minor way, and he was glad of distraction. He let his eyes travel down a page, at random, like a man trying out a lucky dip.

He read that Democritus thought cheerfulness was the goal of life, and disapproved of sex because it meant that consciousness was overwhelmed by pleasure. He read this twice in an absent-minded way and sighed. As he was neither concentrating nor reading in any particular order he turned back a page.

"Matter is not unchanging substance," he read, "but simply a way of grouping events." His interest sharpened. Some events apparently belonged to a group that could be regarded as material things, others such as light rays could not. "It is events that are the stuff of the world." Tycho stared at the page. His hair lay like limp, blond embroidery silk on his babyish forehead.

"Wobbling events though!" he said aloud, almost as if he were supplementing or even correcting the statement in the book with a fuller statement of his own. Then he raised his blue eyes and looked along the street rather as if a fiery angel might be coming towards him. The separate worlds of thought and feeling seemed on the point of rushing together so that he would stop feeling like two people jammed into the same skin, and become the same man, thinker and feeler melted together.

Nothing happened. People moved in their street-dance in and out of each other, from one event to the next. "Cheerfulness is the goal of life," Tycho repeated aloud and, feeling touched and cheered by the thought, smiled and actually laughed, and began practising cheerfulness while he waited for Angela to appear again.

9

FOREIGN RELATIONS

Moving in under the sign bearing her father's name, Angela, falling under his blessing as it were, found herself in what seemed to be an elegant warehouse. She was surrounded by inscrutable objects, things that would only mean something when incorporated into unknown systems of filtration or insulation. After the first surprise, things like camera parts became recognisable, while others remained obscure. Nevertheless, Angela studied them all with eager interest, half-believing she had a share in them, as if an affinity for certain agencies could be inherited in the blood.

The office, according to a neat, clear notice, was on the next floor. Avoiding an attendant who came towards her, probably anxious to sell her a filtration system, Angela went upstairs and found herself in an airy reception room with a carpet of rusty red. Behind the desk a blonde woman looked up and raised her eyebrows. She wore a pale-pink trouser suit and had her platinum-blonde hair twisted in a spiralling knob on top of her head, so that she looked like a long, delicious, pink drink with rich cream on the top.

"May I help you?" she asked.

"Well, maybe," Angela said, and then, feeling young and rough when she wanted to feel sophisticated, put it more formally. "Possibly you can. I want to speak to Mr Chase, please."

"He's with someone at the moment," said the woman. "Would you like to wait?"

"Just for a little bit," Angela said, astonished to find herself both nervous and clumsy. She sat down in one of the chairs and looked at a magazine, just as if she were waiting for the dentist. Almost at once she realised that the receptionist was stealing little glances in her direction, pretending her interest was only absent-minded.

Exhilarated, Angela thought it proved that the likeness between herself and Roland Chase was really there. Other people could see it. Tycho had seen it, of course, but she and Tycho had had a lot of practice at seeing the same things, so he didn't altogether count.

A light, modern, science-fiction telephone peeped plaintively in the voice of an uneasy bird. A call was allowed in behind the closed door, natural wood, grandly varnished and glossy. Angela heard another phone giving an answering call in the unknown room beyond and then fall silent as it was presumably answered. A little later the door opened, and a small, brisk man bustled out, talking over his shoulder to someone. He shut the door behind him.

"See you next week, Myra," he said. The phone piped up again. This time, as the receptionist put the call through, she turned to Angela.

"What name shall I say?" she said, smiling quite nicely. "It's about a job, is it?"

Angela did not have a chance to reply. The door opened. Roland Chase himself came out.

"Myra!" he said. "My mother's on the way up. Can you invent some urgent business for me about five minutes after she gets here." Then he saw Angela, and stared silently at her, expressing neither dismay nor horror. They were no longer separated by a public space where their meeting might just be accidental but across the width of his own reception room. Angela thought he grew pale, but later she thought she might have been the one to change colour. Myra, too, stared at her with open inquisitiveness. Angela felt so full of emotion that she was, for once, hardly able to speak or move. She just looked at Roland Chase as if, like the Little Mermaid, she had no voice and must make him love her with her beautiful body, her graceful walk and lovely eyes.

My father, thought Angela. I'm here with my father.

Roland Chase finished his internal debate.

"All right!" he said. "I'll give you a few minutes. Come on in."

Angela walked into the office that lay beyond the door. At last she had come to her source, the spring of her life, a life that had wound and lashed like Dry Creek Road, with Dido, a cliff on one side, but nothing except an airy abyss on the other. She walked over the rusty-coloured carpet and stood before a desk that reminded her of other desks, desks of teachers at school, desks she had had to stand in front of over and over again, waiting for judgement. Now she waited for judgement once more.

"Well," said Roland Chase, "I suppose you're Dido May's child, are you? Get it off your chest, whatever it is, and then please, please leave me alone. I'm becoming irritated with these accidental-on-purpose encounters and it's much better for both of us to stay well apart."

Angela had half-expected him to say some such thing, but not quite in this tone of voice. Besides, she found it chilling to be referred to as "Dido May's child", as if Dido had to be distinguished from many other Didos by her surname, and as if she herself was such an uncertain quantity that he had not even known whether she was a girl or a boy, and barely knew even now.

"It's all right," she said, trying to use the sort of voice that would fit in with a tennis-court and swimming-pool way of life, but sounding odd and affected in her own ears. "I don't want anything."

Roland Chase looked both angry and amused. "I should say not," he said. "We're talking about a mere possibility. After all I'm not the only red-headed man in the world, and from what I seem to remember, your mother *did* have a wide circle of acquaintances."

Angela felt herself blushing as if he had insulted some very private part of herself, for he had effortlessly revived a hidden, sad guilt that she existed at all. Also for the first time in years she felt gawky and angular, lumpish and overdone, with clumsy feet.

"But you *are* my father," she said.

"As far as I'm concerned I have no children," he told her and smiled a smile as mechanical as if it were a puppet's smile, brought about by tugging a hidden string. "You look as if you've been well looked after, so go home and concentrate on being grateful for that." His voice became kind and persuasive. "It's simple common sense," he added, almost winningly, but Angela had been told common sense was a neat, misleading circle, whereas truth was slightly elliptical and not simple at all.

"Don't you ever wonder how we're getting on?" Angela cried.

"Never!" he declared and repeated it twice, shaking his head slowly. "Never, never!"

"We've been very poor," she said severely. "Even though you paid us money, we've struggled hard a lot of the time." He looked puzzled, and then very intrigued.

"Paid you money?" he said. "To her credit Dido has never once asked for any. I've never paid her a cent."

"But she said you did!" Angela blurted out. He shook his head, frowning with his eyes, the corners of his mouth turned up in a puzzled and unwilling smile.

"I would never admit any responsibility," he said at last. "It's not the sort of thing I ever admit. Anyhow, I always took it to mean she wasn't sure who the father was."

His comments were still clinical, but his inquisitiveness had deepened. He could not hide a cool but strong interest in her, and in Dido too. Unwilling to ask directly in case he gave her encouragement, he waited alertly for her to tell him more.

"Try being enigmatic!" said a voice in her ear, but of course it was not really in her ear. It was a voice out of memory. It was the voice of Tycho Potter.

Angela lowered her head, and smiled with her lips closed. She felt her eyelashes brush her hot cheeks.

"I've stood outside your house and looked in at you," she said, and that was enough to touch him in a way that mattered, as he realised she could invade his private life, could walk up his drive, knock on the panelled door, pat the red retriever and reveal herself to whomever answered. She could appear, dressed for tennis, beside his tennis court, racquets under her arm, looking very much a daughter of the family.

"Now listen carefully!" he said. "You keep away from my home. There's less for you there than there is here – and there's nothing here. This almost amounts to blackmail, you know, and I shouldn't hesitate to get police protection."

Angela hastened to be conciliatory rather than enigmatic.

"I'd never really tell your wife or family," she declared. "I promise I wouldn't. I just wanted to – to meet you."

"You obviously don't know very much about me," he said. "I admit I was married briefly about five years ago – but never before and never again. You should do your research thoroughly. There's no way you can get at me through that sort of threat."

"Threat!" exclaimed Angela, screwing up her face with

bewilderment. She badly wanted to be enigmatic again, but what had just been said suddenly exploded with nightmarish new possibilities. "I'm not threatening you." Then, without a pause, she asked. "Not married? Dido said you were. She said you had three kids."

Roland Chase made a contemptuous sound.

"Have it out with Dido!" he said. "It's nothing to do with me."

Angela had been prepared for many things, for all sorts of drama, for certain kinds of rejection, but everything she expected had always been touched with tenderness, openly acknowledged, or made itself felt in spite of ritual attempts at concealment. Now a huge gear in past time grated and meshed with another, and other wheels, hitherto disconnected and stationary, began to grate painfully too – and to turn. Memories of their first poverty became abruptly eloquent – the shed behind the old man's house, the collapsing cot, Dido crying in the night – not crying for love, but for lack of it. She could remember weary climbs up the hill, when she carried pine cones in a basket, and Dido dragged fallen branches to be sawn up on the edge of the verandah. She could remember Dido whistling and kneeling, cleaning the school lavatories at the same school where she, Angela, had gone as a pupil in due course, and where, on her first day, Tycho, like a moonlit goblin, watching her from under his fringe of silver-white hair (not yet darkened to its present pale yellowish colour) had offered to lend her his felt pens. She also remembered the day Dido and she had bought dye at the chemist's shop at the foot of Dry Creek Road and had spent the weekend dyeing things in the old copper kettle. What excitement when the clothesline blossomed out with scarlet and sky-blue sheets, forest-green pillowcases, purple tea towels. How lovely to be a bright pink, ice cream girl at bedtime, the old pyjamas transformed, a little streaky like the best ice cream but delicious, and made all new again. These banners of defiance had danced against the blue sky up at the top of Dry Creek Road flapping a message over the city, but Roland Chase had never read it. He had never once looked in their direction. Some trace of these instantaneous memories must have shown on her face for a moment, for at last Roland Chase hesitated and asked a human question.

"It hasn't been too bad, has it?" he asked quite gently, and it was an invitation to tell a little of her story, and something of Dido's along with it. "I wouldn't have been an asset, you know."

"You've got asparagus tastes," Dido had once exclaimed crossly, sitting beside her, trying to coax her with stories and games to eat her cabbage and wild parsley. Some days, apart from cabbage and wild parsley there had only been porridge to eat.

"I couldn't be bothered going into town today," Dido had said carelessly, but Angela suddenly knew it was because she had just not had the money, and porridge-days had been much more desperate than Dido had allowed her to believe. Everything made a different sense and Angela, feeling it was all a dreadful mistake, nevertheless knew at last she was understanding something unexpected but true.

"Oh, we've never really needed anyone else," Angela said. "We were always strong." (*Stronger than you,* she managed to imply by making her voice scornful.) "But of course you didn't know that, did you?"

"It sounds as if Dido's led you on a bit, however," he said, and she saw with pleasure she had stung him, though she could not be quite sure how. There was no point in trying to answer his jibe, for Angela had no answers. All she could think of was something Dido had said in answer to Angela's own questioning perhaps three weeks earlier, and she repeated it now.

"Dido says if we'd been with you we'd have been masked from being our true selves," she said. "You would have stood between us and the storm, but we've faced the storm and won as ourselves. We've been fine. I've never needed a father. I was just curious."

This was true in one way, but it was also a terrible lie, for as she said it she felt through the numbness that had held her in its power the beginnings of anguish.

"I was curious, that's all," she repeated firmly, "and I thought you might be too."

"I've never ever been remotely curious," he answered, returning to his colder voice. "Tell me, does Dido know you're here?" Angela now began to consider abusing him. She felt she needed the relief of swearing and she was sickened by their polite, cold game when straightforward swearing seemed so clean and honest. But at that moment the door opened without a preliminary knock, and a glamorous, elderly woman sidled into the room, resplendent in a jade-green suit, her hair rinsed a rusty colour. Wonderful shoes softly embraced feet at the end of thin legs. Over one arm hung a squashy leather handbag, and on the end of the arm was a hand whose nails resembled oval drops of blood. This woman, skinny as a whippet, pointed a bright and dog-like face at Angela, then turned and pointed at Roland Chase, having given Angela a brief view of eyes made up with eyeliner, eye shadow and mascara and a mouth like a scarlet scar folded in on itself, the lips edged with tiny lines, fine as hairs into which the lipstick had run, blurring its outline slightly.

"Now, Ro, you can't keep me waiting outside," the woman said brightly. "I don't care if you've got the President of the Reserve Bank in here. I just won't let you get away with it. I am your mother after all."

Roland Chase had become extremely upset although he tried not to show it. He sighed and pretended to straighten a few straight papers on a perfectly straight desk.

"I wasn't expecting you quite yet," he said.

"I rang the taxi right after I rang you," she said. "I don't mind waiting until five, but then I want you to drive me to the Robinsons and to come in for a drink. They contacted me earlier and asked us to call and they've asked us before, so many times, too. You can be civil for once and just put off whatever dolly-bird you've lined up for the cocktail hour."

"Dolly-bird!" exclaimed Roland Chase scornfully, but Angela could see he was embarrassed by his mother, just as she was sometimes embarrassed by Dido when she used some ancient slang expression as if it were still modern.

"I think that's all," he added, not to his mother but to Angela. "I don't think we need to talk about any of this any more. You must go."

His tone was so forbidding that his mother turned and looked at Angela closely.

"Oh dear," she said brightly. "He doesn't sound very friendly, does he?"

"He sounds like a real jerk, and that's what he is," Angela said. "I was just telling him." Something terrible was happening to her, something deep inside her had started to bleed so that she thought she could actually feel the blood come up into her mouth, thick as syrup and sour-tasting. For a second she wondered if her heart had actually broken, not because she had lost a father, but because at the same time she was also losing the mother she was used to. Dido had never been loved, and never made any noble sacrifice for love, and she herself was just another accidental person who might even have been aborted if abortions had been legally obtainable in the past. Her new, unsuspecting grandmother stared at her with surprise, and then began to suspect, with the changing expression of someone seeing an improbable prophecy come true before her eyes.

"Who are you?" she asked. "Ro, who is it...?"

"It's Dido May's daughter," he said, staring at his mother

with a resentment Angela could recognise but could not understand.

"However, you'll know all about that, won't you?" he added mysteriously. "She's on her way out." Angela could see that he had made up his mind to torment his mother a little bit and was going to use her to do it. "If I *am* your father (which I don't for one moment admit, I hasten to add), this must be your grandmother, and these days she's constantly complaining over her lack of grandchildren, though she was never enthusiastic about having them in the past. Mother, now's your chance to tell her about your visit to Dido, way back before she was born."

"Don't be so bitter, Ro," the woman cried furiously. "I meant everything I did for the best. You're very cruel to me." She turned to Angela and there, plain to see, was the beginning of a quivering eagerness that turned Angela cold, for she had come looking for a father, not a grandmother. As she stared, nonplussed, Roland Chase said to his mother, "I can't introduce you. I don't even know the girl's name."

"Angela," Angela said. "My name's Angela May." It was told at last. She might even hear her father speak her name. But both man and woman exclaimed sharply, their expressions altering, his becoming one of dismay, hers an expression of surprise at first, changing mysteriously to something like delight, though Angela could not tell why.

"That's *my* name!" the woman said incredulously, putting out her hand with its nails like drops of blood, the hand of a true blood relation. "You're named after me."

"Try being enigmatic!" Tycho would have said, did say, alive in her memory like part of her. "It's just a wobble. Open *The Catalogue of the Universe*. Think of stars: say the name Aldebaran! Remember the moon's shadow racing across the world during a total eclipse. Don't lose your temper."

But now the woman began to weep, and wept so easily, Angela understood she had had years of practice.

"For God's sake, Mother..." said Roland Chase. Nothing Angela had said moved him with anything like the embarrassment brought on by this easy flood of tears. As for Angela, she did not lose her temper. At that moment she simply wanted her own mother badly and turned for the door.

"Don't go, don't go," the woman said, putting out her hand again, but Angela ignored her. "Ro, you can't just let her walk out like that!"

"I hope you're satisfied," Roland snapped at her. "You've made an entrance. Now how about an exit?"

Angela did not turn. She went past the woman in the pink suit and down the stairs, through the warehouse, out of the door, under the sign, and at last on to the open street. Though it looked much the same as when she had left it, it was now an entirely different place. While she had talked to her father in another kingdom, a hundred earthly years had gone by, and someone had stolen the world and put a hasty imitation in its place, clever enough in its own way, but still quite easily seen through. In this unreal world a scrap of paper, a dandelion pushing out through a crack between the footpath and the gutter, the crack itself, were suddenly as meaningful as a man, woman or child. Nothing was insignificant. Nothing could be overlooked. Angela stood there, overwhelmed, while the city streamed around her, and then stared down at her hands, anxious to check up on her own skin. She had washed them and put cream on them that morning, had filed a broken nail, but now they belonged to someone else, a morning person who had just ceased to exist. She was quite different from what she had imagined herself to be, not the child of love but the child of betrayal and deception, and even her name was no longer her own, but belonged to the whippet with the red nails who had had it first.

Further down, on the opposite side of the road, Tycho's car was plainly visible, and she moved towards it without particularly wanting to see him, or to see anyone really. It was just that she had to go in some direction. As she went she found that she was muttering the names of things, thinking that if she named them they might jump back into their familiar state, instead of standing out so strangely.

"Wall, concrete, parking meter," she said. "Window, word, telephone box." And as she said this, her hand in her jeans pocket encountered some coins. She took it out, unbent the fingers, and there in her palm were three two-cent pieces, a ten-cent piece and a button. She had enough money to make a phone call.

Dido's number at work was not engaged. She asked for her in a voice as hoarse as if she had been shouting all day at a school sports day.

"Is that you Angela, love?" cried Mrs Cobbett who worked with Dido in the film-hire shop. "You sound as if you've got a cold. Your mum's right here."

Dido's voice said casually, "Hello, honeybear – what's up?"

Angela could not reply. She just listened intently, willing Dido to speak again, hoping that the voice would be familiar and there would be something there she could recognise and begin to belong to again. But the voice sounded tinny and distant, and squeezed small.

"Are you OK?" asked Dido. "Angela?" And then, "Come on. I know you're there."

"I saw him," Angela said at last. "I went there and I saw him. My father. Great romantic Roland Chase! But he's the real bastard, not me!"

It was Dido's turn to be silent.

"I know you're there!" Angela said derisively. "Why did you tell me all those lies? I went to see him and I made a fool of myself."

"Where are you now?" Dido asked.

"What do you want to know for?"

"Well, I don't want to talk about this over the phone. I want to come and get you in the car and take you home where we can talk properly."

"You've had years to talk to me," Angela screamed. She heard her own screaming with relief. It was all right for Tycho to tell her to be enigmatic, or to comfort herself with the general strangeness of things – Angela could not do this.

Only when she saw people stop and turn, staring at the telephone box with disquiet and even fear, did things begin to grow ordinary again, and she felt, at last, that the outside world was acknowledging her once more.

"Where are you?" Dido repeated. "Tell me how to get to you."

"Get in the car then," Angela began "and do what I tell you..." She had no real idea what she was about to say only that it would be something very terrible. "Get into the car and drive up Dry Creek Road and – and *be* a blood sacrifice if you want to. You've had plenty of practice! Dive off into space. I don't care. I don't want any parents. I don't want ever to have been born."

She slammed the receiver down and leaned back against the wall of the phone booth, shaking so much she had to hug herself to hold herself together. The relief of having discharged her anguish in words was so great that, for a moment, she couldn't think properly. Then a different fear seized her. She wanted to take the words back. She searched in her pocket, but there were no more two-cent pieces, and she thumped the glass of the booth so that it rang a dull note. Few things were so irrevocable as hanging up the phone in a phone box. She prepared to thump the glass again, thinking her hand might go right through it this time. She would bleed to death out there in the open street, and Roland Chase would read about it next day in the paper and be stricken with remorse. No, he wouldn't; that was just a romantic notion. She'd have to live long enough to tell her story with her dying breath to the ambulance men who would, in turn, tell reporters. It would be in all the papers and everyone would despise him. His business associates would snub him...

But someone caught her hand as she held it high, and she turned to find herself seized, not by a policeman or a concerned passer-by, but by little Tycho Potter looking terrified.

"You let me go, Big Science!" Angela cried.

"What's happened?" he asked her. "What are you on about? People are looking."

"Get away if I embarrass you!" shouted Angela, trying to shake herself free, but she was unable to do so. He advanced into the phone booth, still holding her wrist and for the first time they both realised that, though he was shorter than she was, he was actually much stronger. He pressed her against the glass, saying as he did so, "What happened?"

"None of your business!" Angela said. "Let me go or I'll flatten you."

"Go on then!" he said. But he held her arms and she was helpless.

"You can't, can you?" he said, and laughed with surprise. "I'll let you go, but not because I'm scared," he told her, and released her, standing back as much as the closeness of the telephone booth would allow, smiling feebly at people still staring in through the glass, wondering what was going on and whether to interfere or not.

"Being so *clever*," Angela said fiercely, "you were right

about Roland Chase. He was horrible. OK? Another top mark? And I've just had the most awful fight with Dido. We'll never get over it."

"I'll drive you home," offered Tycho.

"It's not that sort of fight," Angela said. "Not the sort you go home after. Just get out and leave me alone. I don't want you being bloody reasonable all over the place. Just leave me to wobble off on my own, will you?"

Tycho stared at her. Someone banged impatiently on the door of the telephone box.

"All right!" he said at last, "but I'll tell you two things first. I don't know what's happened, but I do know this – whatever your father thinks – if he *is* your father, that is – your mother loves you." The words were stiff but defiant, as if Tycho knew he was offering yet another piece of unwelcome information. "And *I'm* crazy about you," he added as they stared woodenly at one another. "You're all I think about when you're not there," he went on in a matter-of-fact way, as the banging on the door was repeated, "and you're all I think about when you are. So there!"

"To hell with that!" Angela said, angry and bewildered. "What do you want me to do? Blush and fall all over you? Forget it."

Tycho shrugged.

"You're still what you said you were – a child of love, that's all," he said in the same bustling, efficient voice. Then he frowned, began feeling his pockets, and finally took out a folded ten-dollar note which he placed on the coin box.

"That's for a taxi – or – or something. I don't know," he said rather desperately. "Don't get *stuck*." Angela took a deep breath and he raised his hands in front of his face thinking she might be about to strike him. Then he took them down.

"All right, take a swing at me, if it makes you feel any better," he said. But Angela just stared at him, without any expression he could recognise.

"Well," he said rather foolishly, "I'm going back to my car." Then he began joking in the familiar way, but it was tragic joking at heart. "I'm really of noble English parents," he said, "but I'm going to live out the rest of my life with the great grey apes." And he gave a whooping, yodelling cry, backed away, turned and left her standing in the phone box. She had believed herself beyond feeling anything, but Tycho had surprised her.

"Here, what's going on?" asked a cross man. "Can't you find somewhere else to have your fun and games. This is a public telephone box, you know."

"Oh well, it's all yours now," Angela said, stepping out so he could step in, staring after Tycho, who was climbing into the car across the road.

"Hey, Big Science!" she called uncertainly, and he waved one hand back over his shoulder as he unlocked the door of the car. The cross man came out of the telephone box, and shook the ten-dollar note irritably at her.

"You just don't care, do you?" he said. "Kids!" he added in disgust.

"Thanks!" she said, and took it, still watching Tycho get

into his car without turning his head. He started the engine, pulled out into the stream of traffic and drove away at once, for at that time of day when traffic was leaving town, his side of the street was almost empty. He did not look or wave again. Angela stared after him until he turned around the next corner and was lost to sight.

10

MRS POTTER ROLLS
A CIGARETTE

Tycho had always been close to his mother even as he grew older. It was only recently he had begun to find himself keeping more and more secrets from her because they seemed to have nothing to do with the safe life she wanted for him – a life without pain, sorrow or despair, contented rather than ecstatic. Still there must have been an early time when she wanted more than safety for her children, and the evidence for this was in his strange middle name, the one he had chosen to be called by when he was quite small. They had all had a choice, but who could say why Africa had chosen to be called Africa rather than Rosemary, and Richard Richard rather than November.

When asked why she had given such strange second names to her children, Mrs Potter always said she'd given them their first names for everyday use, and their second names because she had liked the sound of the words, but sometimes it seemed that she had given them choice at the very beginning of their lives. If they wanted to, they could choose the strange name and follow it, like the golden ball in a fairy tale, wherever it might lead them. Thus Richard might finally come to heel, and Tycho end by measuring vast explosions in infinity.

Tycho did not go home for a while. He drove up on to the hills, not very far from where they had worked the previous morning and stared solemnly down at the city. Somewhere down there Angela was stalking along, an old romance shredding away from her like a ruined skin. Beyond the city he could see the mountains where, two years ago, Angela and he, brought together by accident, had watched a total eclipse of the sun and had felt the shadow of the moon, darker than the twilight in which they stood, pass over them as quickly as the blink of a giant eyelid. They had come out from the shadow as friends. Now Tycho was uncertain whether or not he was being a true friend to Angela, having faith that she would find her own way home, or whether he was simply a coward.

He came back to his own house to find his parents and Richard deep in a conversation about what wine they should take to Africa's anniversary party.

"Red is much more stylish these days," Richard was insisting. "Fizzy white is definitely out."

"Oh, but I love it! It seems so festive," Mrs Potter argued, "and I *do* like bottles with gold tops."

"Take some of that ginger beer you made and shove some gold paper around the top of that," Richard advised her. "You know, the stuff out in the garage. Now that's so festive that there's only about a quarter of an inch left when all the fizzing dies down. Pure celebration with a bottle around it."

Mr Potter was sitting by the kitchen window with a travel brochure in front of him. Within a week he and his wife were planning a visit north to the Sounds and he was reading about the various things they could do there, such as taking launch trips or going fishing. He smiled to himself, anticipating sun and sea which was waiting to be enjoyed before the Christmas rush set in.

"Hudson's had plenty of free booze at our place," he remarked without looking up. "I'm looking forward to having some at his expense."

"I'm sorry to say it," said Richard, looking pleased, "but there's a mean streak in Hudson. I hope Hamish hasn't inherited it."

"Oh well, be fair, Richard!" cried Mrs Potter, prepared to defend Hudson as long as he remained safely married to Africa. "Drink causes so much trouble, and this is an anniversary party, not one of your orgies."

"*My* orgies?" exclaimed Richard indignantly. "Mine? When can I afford an orgy?" But his parents were not paying attention to him. "Pity!" he mumbled. "Well, let's go, Dad."

He and Mr Potter set off for the nearest bottle store. Tycho sat at the kitchen table, barely hearing the voices that came and went around him. He was wondering if he should have followed Angela in some way, imagining himself disguised, sidling around town after her, ready to leap out and defend her in her possible hour of need. He imagined her in the power of yesterday's tattooed gang, saw himself confronting them and quoting, "Nothing exists but atoms and the void." A jagged white comic-book star exploded in the air. "POW!" said the black letters in its heart. A villain would fall to the ground, as if Democritus had disabled him with a kung-fu chop. Tycho laughed aloud, desolate and amused in his own kitchen. Then he rubbed the back of his neck, pulled a face and swore softly. How could anyone help Angela? For her, the wobble had suddenly turned into a fall, and if he had jumped after her there would have been no one to hold out a hand when the fall was over. Besides, she would always have been falling ahead of him.

"What did you say?" asked his mother, turning.

"Nothing!" Tycho said. She came and sat down in the chair Mr Potter had left empty, and turned the brochure over as he had done. But, unlike her husband, she was not concerned with their holiday.

"Isn't this nice?" she said, meaning the quietness that Mr Potter and Richard had left behind them. Early evening sunlight shone through the leaves of the Virginia creeper hanging down over the edge of the porch. The kitchen filled with a quivering, dappled shade.

"Mum," Tycho said. "I don't think I'll go tonight. There's an occultation of two of Jupiter's moons and I..."

"Oh, Tycho," cried his mother reproachfully. "You can see Jupiter's moons at any time of the week."

"No, I can't," Tycho said, trying to make an occultation sound rarer than it actually was.

"Tycho, I haven't lived with you for all these years without knowing something about Jupiter and its moons," his mother said sharply. "And anyway, isn't Jupiter too low in the sky to be worth observing at present?"

"I can see it between the houses," Tycho said, glad that this at least was true, but his mother gave him a quick look that reminded him of a blackbird, cocking its head and looking sideways on hearing a rustle in the undergrowth.

"It's that girl, isn't it?" she asked.

"Angela," said Tycho. "Not 'that girl'."

"Oh, Angela, then!" Mrs Potter sounded as if she hated the name. "Tycho, Africa would love to see you, and I'd like you to come along with us and make a real family occasion of it." Her voice grew confiding. "You see, I feel she needs family support at present – she's finding life a little bit difficult..."

"Mum, Africa won't notice whether I'm there or not," Tycho answered patiently. But he was beginning to feel selfish – not towards Africa, but towards his mother. "Anyhow I haven't got her a present."

"I gave you ten dollars this morning," Mrs Potter cried out. When she was indignant she looked quite pretty, her eyes wide and sparkling, her face a little tightened with anger. "What has happened to that ten dollars?"

"I spent it. I gave it away," Tycho said. "Mum, I'm sorry," he declared immediately. "I didn't have any choice. I'll get it back all right." But he felt as if he were five years old, sent to buy bread and coming home with the change all spent on comics and ice cream.

"None of you – none of you – thinks of anyone these days except yourselves," Mrs Potter declared in such a fierce, sad voice that Tycho was horrified at her distress, and at himself for having caused it. Nevertheless, he would not give in.

"I do think of you," he said urgently. "I truly do – I just don't think of Africa very much."

"You could have thought more of me," said Mrs Potter. "Maybe I'm wasting my time, but you people – my family – you're all I've got apart from china painting." She stood up and looked at Tycho almost contemptuously, but then her expression softened, and she sighed and sought for consolation.

Mrs Potter had her own way of living dangerously. She had an unlikely vice. Once or twice during the day she would smoke a private cigarette, and believed that she made up for her lapse by turning this small fault into a craft. Mrs Potter rolled her own. Preparing the cigarette was part of the ritual by which she calmed and comforted herself. She now collected her lighter, a tin of tobacco and some papers from the top of the fridge, where they sat among a collection of unrelated kitchen objects – an electricity bill weighted down by a little green bottle with a single overblown rose in it, a slightly larger bottle of wine vinegar, a tin lid filled with ashes from an earlier cigarette, and an ashtray holding two buttons, a safety pin and two hairclips.

"My heart sank when you first brought her home, I must admit," she said, sitting down again. "She looks like trouble."

"Probably Hudson's mother thought the same thing when she first saw Africa coming up the drive," Tycho argued. His mother hesitated, raising her eyebrows, pursing her lips. Just for a moment, a different personality seemed as if it might be about to break through, something less cosy, even slightly raffish, much more the personality of a woman who rolled her own cigarettes. Perhaps it was to placate this tougher self that she smoked at all.

"Who can say?" she asked unexpectedly. "Mind you, I still say Hudson was lucky to get Africa. She's out of his class really. But if you mean Angela and Africa have got a little bit in common – well, yes, I'll accept that. But Tycho, be fair – you can only make allowances for just so many people." Tycho watched her management of her cigarette with pleasure, enjoying the contrast between her cool, quick folding of the fragile, fluttering paper around the tobacco (something she could do with one hand like a shearer or a road man), and the flowery summer suit and the apricot frill of her blouse. She ran the tip of her tongue along the gummed edge, like a cat licking butter.

"She really likes me," Tycho insisted. In one way he did not want to talk about Angela, but in another he did not want to talk about anything else. "I've been chosen. I'm it!" he said, as if he were talking about a game. "I don't mean by Angela. By something else."

"Chosen?" Mrs Potter said sharply. "What on earth do you mean by that?"

"It's a sort of doom," Tycho tried to explain, but found

himself putting his hand half across his mouth, muffling the words in an attempt to tell and not tell at the same time. "We started school on the same day. I thought she was just so – well, so pretty," he exclaimed. "Her hair was such a wonderful colour, like sunset. I felt really pleased to be in a room with such a pretty... object. I lent her my felt pens." He looked up and saw his mother staring at him with a deeper dismay than she had ever shown before. "I didn't feel sexy about her," he hastened to add, but rather doubtfully.

"I should hope not, at five!" Mrs Potter now became vaguely affronted.

"Well, people say quite little kids do," Tycho pointed out, "and kids make a lot of jokes about it. They shout and groan in the pictures when people kiss. I mean, they know it's disreputable, don't they?"

"Between people who truly love one another, it's very beautiful," said Mrs Potter, smiling but prim. She had used that same phrase when reassuring Tycho about the astonishing facts of life many years earlier.

"Well, what if only *one* person is in love?" Tycho asked, half-teasing her, but also because he wanted to hear her theory. "Is that only half as beautiful? Do you have to have input from both sides, or can one person make it beautiful even if the other person isn't interested?"

"Don't get smart with me," said his mother crisply. "You children spoil everything with smartness and that dreadful computer language."

"But all the same – Angela's what I remember from my

first day at school," Tycho said. "That, and the wonderful cake you specially put in my lunch," he added. "And even then it took me ages to get to know her, because she's in one of the groups and I'm in another." ("I'm on my own," he should have said, for real accuracy.)

"Well, you've always been one of the clever ones," said Mrs Potter a little complacently. "You've all done well at school, you children."

The cigarette hung a little on her lower lip. Tycho and Richard always enjoyed seeing it do that. It was a thin, uneven cigarette and, quite innocently, she looked like an uncertain beginner smoking a joint, and doing it wrongly.

"Most people would want to be beautiful rather than clever though," Tycho said. "If we had the choice, that is."

"Oh, Tycho, believe me – beauty is only skin deep," Mrs Potter said, with as much sincerity as if she had worked this out only the moment before.

"Yes, well, that's more than deep enough," answered Tycho, who had had a lot of time to think about that particular saying.

"You poor dear!" his mother said. "We've all been interested in unsuitable people, but it *does* pass, you know."

This was no consolation to Tycho, who did not want his feelings to pass, only that they should be wildly satisfied.

"Well, say what you like, I think you've got nice eyes," Mrs Potter suddenly commented with the air of one announcing an unlikely discovery. Tycho made a gesture of such impatience that she suddenly demanded with a new and inexplicable anguish, "What's the matter? Aren't I allowed to say what I think? You're my son. Can't I say something nice about you?"

But Tycho wanted to be as beautiful as Lucifer, and instead, he sat here in the kitchen with his mother telling him he had nice eyes, and somewhere out in the city Angela was wandering quite out of control – unless, after all, she had changed her mind and gone home. He let himself glance casually at the phone, squatting in its corner beyond the fridge like a disinterested toad. He had let her go. He had not even turned when she called his name across the street.

"I don't mean that there aren't some nice things about her," Mrs Potter persisted. Tycho thought of walking out of the room, but he was trapped in the kitchen chair by guilt towards his mother. "She's nicely spoken for one thing, but there's something – how can I put it – something a little bit *blatant* about her."

"Isn't there just!" Tycho agreed, with a reluctant grin. "But, Mum, it is blatant – sex, I mean – when it's working well. It's not – well, it's not ashamed of itself, is it? Remember Morris-the-cat?" For Morris-the-cat, prior to her hasty operation, had been a voluptuous creature, luring suitors on, then spitting and rebuffing them, slinking along behind the bean sticks followed by a procession of enchanted toms, all compelled by her seasonal power.

"You can't compare people with cats." Mrs Potter sounded indignant again. "I just don't think it ought to be showy. Now, that shirt she was wearing the day before yesterday... from some angles you could see right through it, and I don't think she was wearing much underneath it."

"No," Tycho agreed, having seen that same shirt from many angles during the working day.

"...and those shorts she sometimes wears are so short they show the beginning of her *derrière.*" Mrs Potter paused, looked at him, and then said, smiling plaintively, "but I can see that anything she does is all right by you."

"No – not quite!" Tycho replied. "But she's not here, and whether she wears anything under her shirt or not, she's a friend and I have to stand up for her, don't I?" Then he sighed a little at the two-faced treachery of words.

"Yes, dear." His mother patted his arm, sounding resigned at last. "Tycho – you've got a really nice nature and that's better than looking like Superman any day. Life's a real old puzzle, isn't it?" she went on quickly. "I mean, look at us. We've got so many reasons to be happy that it seems ungrateful not to be happier than we are."

Tycho did not know what to say. "We're not unhappy, are we?" he asked cautiously. "Just a bit fretful at times. But everyone is."

"Oh yes," she agreed, but once again there was a note of contempt in her voice, and Tycho understood that she was as ambitious for great family happiness as he had been, a moment ago, for extreme beauty, and that faint praise was not enough for her either.

"There are the others," she remarked, as the car drove past the window into their little yard. Morris-the-cat leapt on to Tycho's knees and pushed her round head under his idle hand. Tycho scratched the top of her head between her ears and she began to purr, not daintily, but making hoarse, rattling sounds as if the pleasure brought on by his touch was beyond her control.

"It's not just the happiness I wanted for us," Mrs Potter said. "I don't like all this arguing. I know it's a game to you boys, but it's serious, too."

"All games are a little bit serious," Tycho agreed. "If you get involved in sport at school, it isn't long before someone is telling you sport will train you for the challenges of life. Bash! Biff! Zonk! I don't want that sort of life anyway, even if I could get it."

They could hear the slam of the car door.

"Tycho, I'm so afraid Angela is just using you, and you'll be let down and suffer dreadfully," his mother said all in a rush, anxious to say what she had to say before the others came in.

"Using me for what?" asked Tycho. "I wish she would."

"Well – you often have the car," said his mother vaguely.

"Listen – she's not a girlfriend," Tycho said patiently. "There are other boys she likes better. I have to tell you people over and over again. She talks to me a lot, we read and make jokes, but she goes out at night with other boys and probably sleeps with them. I don't know because I don't ask her. If I did she'd tell me. I just don't want to be told."

"There you are then!" Mrs Potter cried in a mystifying triumph as if something had finally been proved. "Tycho, don't let Morris-the-cat climb on to the table, please. You never know where her paws have been. I don't want to whinge at you, but it does seem to me I'm giving my whole life to trying to make other people happy, and then they go chasing off after unhappiness, when anyone with half an eye can see it's a disaster." She got up as she spoke, and stubbed out the end of her cigarette in the tin lid on top of the fridge. As she did this the other, tougher self showed briefly through the soft colours of her make-up once more.

"The old man's better off," Tycho said. "He'd have gone down the drain without you."

"Tycho don't talk about your father that way," Mrs Potter said, glancing out through the window over the sink and across the porch to where Mr Potter and Richard had been brought to a standstill by an argument over an incident involving Richard's driving and a give-way sign.

"I had plenty of room," Richard was saying. "I could see the whole street either way." Mr Potter, unable to drive himself, hated not being in some sort of control of the family car.

"His life is a million times better because of you," Tycho repeated stubbornly. "Anyhow, isn't it a bit wrong to think happiness is all smooth and serene. Isn't it mostly a great energetic struggle – you against the universe – a great whopping opponent, with the referee in its pocket?"

"I don't believe the universe wants us to be miserable, Tycho," Mrs Potter said stubbornly.

"I've got a book called *The Catalogue of the Universe*,"

Tycho said, "and there's not one mention of happiness in it. There are two Tychos, mind you – the crater on the moon, and a star called Tycho's Star. It went supernova in 1572 and the real Tycho measured it and recorded it. They can still detect the effects of the explosion, you know. Why did you call me Tycho?" he asked. "I mean where did you find the name?"

"In a magazine at the doctor's," his mother said, after a moment's thought.

"You plugged my head into an infinite system," Tycho told her as his father and Richard, still arguing, came into the room. "I wish you'd called me Casanova. It might have worked."

"Casanova?" said Mrs Potter seriously. "The Casanova who... Well, that would have been a burden to you at school."

"He was a librarian as well as a stud, you know," Tycho said. "Just my luck to get stuck with the librarian bit."

"We weren't in any great hurry," Mr Potter was saying to Richard. "It wouldn't have done any harm to take it a little more slowly... that's all I'm saying."

"Your cousin Jenny went to library school," Mrs Potter told Tycho, connecting him professionally to Casanova as well as she could. "What did you get, Richard? Show me."

"I got it," said Mr Potter. "It was my money we spent."

"A riot pack," said Richard, meaning that he had bought a large carton holding three litres of wine, "and a proper bottle with a gold top, just for you. Don't let Hudson scoff the lot."

He put the wine down on the kitchen counter and flung one arm around his mother's shoulders. "Aha, old lady! Been on the fags again, have you?"

"Smoking like a chimney!" Tycho said. "What an example to set."

Morris-the-cat purred incessantly, writhed her head under Tycho's hand and kneaded his leg with her paws. She was desperate to be fed. At last she put her paws on his chest, and rubbed her striped, pansy face against his, so that her nose accidentally brushed his mouth and he shivered at the intimate touch.

"Tycho says he isn't coming," Mrs Potter said. "I did want it to be a nice family occasion – all of us together." She looked at him wistfully and Tycho tried to pretend he was unaware of her gaze by looking at the phone.

"Nice family occasion!" Richard cried. "Mum, remember that last holiday we had at Queenstown years ago? Africa, Dad and I did nothing but fight, and Tycho didn't take his nose out of a book from beginning to end. And Africa picked up that really ghastly guy – worse than Hudson – and wanted him included in everything we did."

Mr Potter sat down at the table and looked at his brochure again.

"Hundreds of dollars that holiday cost me," he said.

Mrs Potter put the bottle of wine in the fridge, Morris-the-cat leapt off Tycho's knee and tore across the kitchen, peering anxiously into the enchanted oblong of light the open door revealed. Lines of poetry came back to Tycho.

It was a miracle of rare device,

A sunny pleasure dome with caves of ice.

What Coleridge had described was a fridge from a cat's point of view. Somewhere else in the poem, which was one they had done at school, was a line about a woman wailing for her demon lover. It was not a demon lover that Angela had wailed for in the telephone box, but a father who, though he had never really existed, had vanished into nothing, like a demon king.

"Hundreds of dollars," Mr Potter repeated, "and all Richard remembers is the fighting and Africa's ghastly guy."

"There was that lovely autumn colouring," said Mrs Potter. "He remembers that."

"Not nearly as well as I remember the fighting," Richard said simply. "I'll bet Tycho only remembers that book about the Voyager One space probe."

"It had just gone past Jupiter," Tycho said.

Mr Potter looked highly dissatisfied with this memory.

"Launch trips – that helicopter ride..." he prompted them. "I saved up for years so that we could go."

"I do remember now," Tycho hastened to add, pleased to be honestly grateful. "Of course I do."

"Mind you, in terms of financial outlay the Voyager One space probe must have been even more expensive than our holiday in Queenstown," Richard said thoughtfully.

"They found eight active craters on Io," Tycho reminded everyone.

"Eight active craters! Just fancy! Well, well!" Mr Potter nodded his head, looking ironically at Tycho.

"Sometimes I think I'll give up on all of you," Mrs Potter said in mock despair. Of all the people in the kitchen only Tycho knew how close her mock despair was to being the real thing.

"You never will!" Richard said, putting his arm around her again. "And just think – Tyke and I may be selfish and parasitic, but that only means we're nice, healthy, normal boys. What more could any home-loving mum want?"

I wonder if Angela has got herself home yet? Tycho thought, staring at the deepening evening beyond the porch.

11

MIDNIGHT APPOINTMENTS

Tycho was not used to being alone. Silence took him by surprise and he found himself walking down the hall looking past open doors into rooms made unfamiliar by quietness. The silent house seemed engaged in a secret debate of its own for, without its people, everything in it – his father's worn slippers under a chair; Richard's camera watching him like an eye from the hall table; his mother's apron, a discarded floral skin hanging on the back of the kitchen door – all took on new meanings. In his own room the walls around his bed now sang to him like a chorus of actual voices and although he was not exactly comforted, he was certainly sustained by their sympathy. They suggested that the true beauty of the world lay in its mystery, which, however, men must struggle to understand.

The Ionian idea that existence might be made understandable, even predictable, because it had an inner order that could be discovered and understood, had been a thrilling thought to Tycho, not because it was new, but because he had kicked it around for a number of years himself without quite knowing what it was. He had first heard this idea described so that he recognised it by Carl Sagan in the television series, *Cosmos*, and had then followed it through various books, increasingly intrigued with its ancient history and the men who had started it moving out into other minds. Thales had first predicted an eclipse; Anaximander had learned to measure time; Anaxagoras had said that "the purpose of life was the study of the sun, the moon and the heavens"; Pythagoras (the triangle man) had thought that the world might be a sphere... These men of olden times had come to their conclusions partly because of their own science, but just as much through imagination. The first scientists had all been imagination men.

Following after them, Tycho discovered a strange thing. It was impossible for explanation to make anything commonplace to him. The more clearly things revealed themselves the more intensely mysterious they became. The very moment when he felt he had things most clearly in his sights was the very moment they silently dissolved back into wonder so he could not dispose of mystery, only move more deeply into it.

And now he had his own silence, he also had to break it.

He went to the telephone and dialled Angela's number. The phone was answered immediately, but it was Dido.

"Isn't she back yet?" were Tycho's first words. He did not even need to say who was speaking.

"No – not yet!" Dido replied. "I've tried all the places she might be. I rang you first of all, but you were still out. To tell you the truth I hoped you were with Angela."

Tycho thought of his mother dressing up to go and visit her own troublesome daughter, saying nothing to him about any phone call and certainly not wanting him involved in Angela's difficulties.

"Did you know she was going round to confront Roland Chase like that?" Dido asked him. She had a light, inconsequential way of talking, and she sounded rather as if she were discussing a character in a book.

"Only this afternoon," Tycho said. "I probably could have guessed though, if I'd thought about it, because of yesterday." Dido did not appear to know about yesterday and didn't ask. "Angela was doing it like a serial story, chapter by chapter, first watching him, and then letting him know she was watching, trying to make him guess who she must be," Tycho told her.

"He must have been terrified," Dido said.

"She wanted him to speak first, but he wouldn't," Tycho then explained.

"No, he wouldn't," Dido agreed. "He was never very bright about people, although naturally I didn't see it at the time. When he was scared or anxious he could get quite nasty though. I did know that. Not that it worried me, because I thought I was a special case. I haven't seen him since I first knew I was expecting Angela."

Tycho did not know what to say.

"Well, I think she wants to kill him," he remarked at last. "He'd better watch out."

"I think she wants to kill me," Dido said. "However, I don't die to order."

Her remote, detached, almost amused voice bothered Tycho.

"Aren't you worried?" he asked bluntly.

"Tycho, I'm worried sick," she answered, and let him hear, at last, something thin and brittle in her cool tone. "I think I ought to ring the police. You and she are always making fun of romance, I know, but really you're both riddled with it – and it's romantic to write yourself off under certain circumstances."

"You mean she might try to kill herself?" Tycho cried. It was a thought that had never crossed his mind.

"I don't think she'd commit suicide – no! She's much too fond of life," Dido said. "She might walk to the top of the cliff and look at the fall, but she'd never jump. What I'm frightened of is that, being at the top of the cliff, she might – oh, I don't know – get drunk and test the edge, say, or even fall over by accident, if you get my meaning."

Tycho had nothing to say to this.

"But I've loved her so much," Dido went on unexpectedly, since she was only speaking to Tycho. "I really have, and I have to have faith in that – in the triumph of love, I suppose. Now there's a romantic cliché for your collection!"

"It must win sometimes," Tycho said, comforted immediately. "Statistically, that is."

"Yes – but not always in the way we most want it to," Dido replied. "Oh well!"

Tycho thought that things must have wobbled dreadfully for Angela's mother.

"I'd better get off the phone in case she rings," he said.

"If I don't hear soon, I'll get in touch with the police and ask them to keep an eye open for her," said Dido, "or go to the top of the cliff myself and look for her – if *I* can work out where it is for Angela. It's in a different place for everyone, isn't it? Let me know if she contacts you, won't you?"

"And you let me know," Tycho said. "I'm alone in the house until late."

He carefully replaced the receiver, went to his room and brought out first his tripod, and then the long box holding the tube and eye-pieces of his telescope. Unfolding the tripod's grasshopper legs, setting the tube on its mounting, he remembered how his father had helped him assemble this amateurish but precious instrument from a Japanese kit-set. During the time of making the telescope, he had been close to his father, had watched him adjust it, over and over again, becoming more and more intrigued and serious over the work. Mr Potter had borrowed tools from a friend to help him get it just right. Then they had taken it out into the garden and pointed it at the moon which had been quarter full. Easily caught, it had swung in the object lens, a white fish of night, but for the first second Tycho had been overwhelmed with disappointment at the imprecision of the image, before remembering that he could focus his telescope and drag shape into what he was seeing.

He turned the little screw slowly, the texture of the white fish altered, and suddenly there was a surface made familiar by many photographs, seen in a flash and then gone again.

He turned the screw minutely back – and at last caught it. The moment became the event. There was the Sea of Crises, with the Sea of Fertility below it and the crater Cleomedes above, just as pictures had shown him, but all laid out on a surface curving to meet him. The glass captured the image and set it in his own eye. There it was – it really was – both outside and inside, a little world hanging in space, a silver apple sliced by a crescent blade of shadow. Tycho, beginning his nightly assignations with this landscape, watched it grow and change, the moon slowly revealing itself, pushing darkness ahead of it, then pulling darkness after it once more. Tonight, two nights after full, the moon would be too bright to be properly looked at, all light and no shadow, and only rising late. When at last it did rise, it came up lopsided, coloured a deep orangey-red, strange and dramatic, casting an orange glow over the city.

Tycho carried his *Catalogue of the Universe* out on to the porch, but he did not start watching Jupiter even though it was falling rapidly down the sky. The city lights would affect the clarity with which he was able to see things; there was a tremor of heat in the air, a promise of summer, ready to distort the images of stars, but Tycho was used to all these disadvantages and not put off by them. He simply sat and thought, filling himself with space and time because that was what he needed to do. It was his own form of meditation. Everything flowed into him and, at last feeling big enough to understand everything that could possibly be understood, stretched up and out with dreams and ideas,

Tycho became giant-like in the dark. ("The purpose of life is the investigations of the sun, the moon and the heavens," offered a voice from the inside market where ideas were bought and sold. "I'll take that one," Tycho said eagerly. "A big hand for Anaxagoras.")

The night spun around him, a vast, slow wheel, and midnight approached. At last he turned his telescope on Jupiter, now framed by two television aerials. On either side of it the telescope showed him four minute pinpricks of light, the Galilean moons. In his telescope they were mere white points, but he knew their names as Io, Callisto and Europa, his sisters, and Ganymede, his brother. He knew about Io's volcanoes, and that she carried a sort of sodium atmosphere close to her, emitting a yellow light almost as if someone had put a lamp-post out near Jupiter, the failed star. He knew that Europa appeared to be encircled in water ice, that Ganymede was probably wrapped in a mantle of methane and ammonia frost, and that Callisto seemed to be covered mostly with soil and wore a bright polar cap. Close to the surface of the planet, beyond the power of his telescope to discover, was the innermost moon, Amalthea, redder than Mars, redder than any known object within the solar system. This variety continually amazed Tycho – this apparently irrational variation. He had lied to his mother about the occultation, but watching those pinpoints of light, he invested them with frost, with polar caps, with volcanoes and water ice, filled in the reddest spot in the solar system and then, looking away, thought about the optical luminosity and X-rays in the constellation in Cassiopeia where an old explosion was still having its effect. Tycho's exploding star was still expanding out, though Tycho de Brahe, the measuring man with the golden nose, was no longer around to measure it.

His mother's clock with the Westminster chimes struck out a sweet midnight. Tycho began to move back into the house, going in on another day from the one on which he had come out. He left *The Catalogue of the Universe* on the porch rail, unbolted the barrel of his telescope and carried it delicately inside where, setting it on the table, he carefully put the eye-pieces back into their box. He was just manoeuvring the tripod through the door, trying to prevent its spiked feet from catching in anything, including Morris-the-cat, when the phone rang and immediately Angela rushed into his mind, displacing the brother and sister moons and the exploding star. The universe rushed away from him so quickly he almost saw the stars redden with the light shift of their violent retreat. Democritus would have despised him. He dropped the tripod, which collapsed like a crippled insect in the doorway, and seized the phone.

It was Richard.

"Clever of you not to come," Richard said. "It hasn't been much of a rave. However, the main thing is Dad's had a bad turn. You know…"

"Is he OK?" Tycho asked anxiously.

"Oh yes – just as usual – a bit dopey now and a headache. It was the full thing. And it's been such a long time since he had one, so it's all a bit depressing. I don't think we'll come home tonight. Africa and Mum have put him to bed, and I'll stay on and sleep on the floor. Africa's got a sleeping bag."

"How can you all fit in?" Tycho asked. "There isn't room."

"Yes, there is," Richard said in a peculiar voice. "Mum and Dad can have the double bed, because Hudson's gone home to his mother." Then he gave an odd squeak over the phone. He was wanting to laugh, but trying not to do so because of something going on in the background.

"What's happening?" Tycho asked. "Can't you tell me?"

"Tomorrow!" Richard said. "It's too complicated now. Just what you might think, though. Hudson's mum upset ours, and then ours upset his, and Hudson and Africa nagged each other all evening..." (someone shouted at him across a room) "and... oh well, just your run-of-the-mill wedding anniversary, I suppose. A proper family get-together. How was your evening?"

"You know what the universe is like," Tycho said. "A lot of stars and inscrutability."

"Terrific. Shove some in the oven for me," Richard said. "I'll have it when I get home. At present I'm disguised as the man of the family and the disguise doesn't fit all that well. It rubs against all my tender parts. You don't mind spending a night on your own, do you?"

"I've got Morris-the-cat," Tycho answered. "You lot stay as long as you like. Give my love to the parents. Poor old man."

"You know how gallant he gets – he's been flirting with his medication," Richard said rather grimly. "OK, Tyke, hang in there! We'll see you soon."

Tycho put the phone down, and then looked at it as if it might be about to make further comment on the messages it had conveyed. Then, as he stood there, he thought he heard his tripod folding itself behind him and turned, his hair prickling with alarm. Behind him in the open doorway stood Angela, picking up the tripod he had dropped there, watching him narrowly as she did so, while under her right arm, held against her body by her elbow so that her hand was left free, was *The Catalogue of the Universe*, which he had left out on the rail in sight of the stars.

12

A STEP UP IN THE WORLD

She looked very disreputable – there was no other word for it – her uncombed hair dull and matted, her face pale enough for dirt to show up on it, not to mention a blue-grey mark on her cheek, as if she had scraped it against a wall. Her eyes were swollen and so defiantly red he knew she had only just stopped crying a moment or two earlier. He could see pearly tracks down her face where her tears had crawled like moon snails. Because he was slightly shorter than she was he saw her raw eyes hooded by shadow. The T-shirt she had worn earlier in the day was gone, her Indian muslin shirt clung to her as if she were wet or electric, so there was no mercy for Tycho in her savage appearance. Although her pallor and swollen eyes were features that might have negated beauty, she seemed nothing less than a wonderful demon of the night, fading everything around her to insignificance.

"Have you got a handkerchief?" she asked, sniffing. "My nose has gone all athletic."

"Running…" Tycho said, feeling in his pockets.

"Well, jogging, anyway," she amended.

He found a very neatly folded soft handkerchief that he had used to wrap the telescope's eye-pieces in. Angela blew her nose as if she really enjoyed doing so. She had never been one for dabbing politely.

"Feel better?" Tycho said, accepting his handkerchief back again rather dubiously. Along with his book, he now saw she held a small, squashy parcel in a purple bag, inscribed with the name of a jeans shop in the city.

"Are you OK?" he said awkwardly. "I mean, I can see you're able to walk and talk and…"

"I'm a bit cold!" she interrupted him. "I left my jacket in your car, and I did something else with my T-shirt." She put the parcel and book down on the end of the kitchen counter.

"Where have you been? You look a real wreck," Tycho asked. "Also you stink a bit, if you don't mind me saying so."

Angela, quite unabashed, sniffed the sleeve of her shirt and grinned slightly. "I do, don't I?" she said. "Sort of sour! I meant to try and wake you up by rapping at the window and crying at the lock, but the light was on and I heard what you were saying on the phone. Are we really alone in the house?"

"Yes," Tycho said. His family problems seemed far away. He found he was actually shaking a little bit. "They're all over at Africa's."

"Well, may I have a shower then?" she asked, "and borrow some clothes of yours – right down to the skin. I'm not too shy to wear your underpants. Your things might more or less fit me."

Tycho thought of his mother with a certain apprehension.

"Saturday tomorrow," he said. "It's the day for clean towels. I'll change mine a day early."

"It's Saturday now!" she said. "No need to break any rules, even."

Tycho fetched her a towel and face flannel.

"Soap – hair shampoo," he said. "Anything else?" He couldn't be quite sure if the excitement that filled him was exhilaration, or his old friend panic.

He went through his cupboard and found a pair of corduroy trousers, a hand-knitted jersey and some underwear, washed and folded away in the big chest of drawers by his mother. He saw the jersey, an old one, had something of his own shape stretched into it. He carried it over to her, whistling under his breath to help him keep some appearance of composure. Angela looked at the trousers critically.

"What about those other ones?" she asked. "Haven't you got those other ones?"

"In the wash," Tycho said. She looked up, smiling a little at his wooden voice. Then she took hold of the front of his shirt and pulled him towards her.

"Don't you try being all laid-back with me," she told him. "I can read you like a book, Big Science."

"I know," said Tycho. "I'm big print and short words. Just don't forget who taught you to read though," he added rather more aggressively.

Angela vanished into the bathroom leaving the door open. "I could read ages before I started talking to you," she shouted.

"Yes, but you didn't know *what* you were reading," he said, going back into the kitchen and beginning to look for the coffee.

"I knew *what* I was reading," she shouted back, "but I just didn't know *all* that I was reading. That's different."

There was a rattle as the sharp spray from the shower hit the plastic curtain, then it turned into a soft shushing sound. Angela had pulled the curtain aside and scrambled under the shower leaving the curtain pulled back.

"What are you doing here?" he asked, and his words brought an echo of *The Sheik* into the Potter kitchen. Angela shouted with laughter.

"Are you not man enough to know?" she called back.

Tycho faced the open hall door and the open bathroom door beyond it.

"It doesn't work," he said softly.

"What?" Angela shouted. "Speak up!"

"It doesn't matter," Tycho said. "I'll tell you when you come out."

But there was something wonderful about this early morning domesticity that filled him with a soft and heady pleasure. He made sandwiches and put them in the sandwich toaster, his mother's Christmas present from Africa. He heated water to make coffee.

"Come and sit on the edge of the bath, and talk to me while I wash my hair," Angela called. "Don't be shy! You don't have to look at me."

Tycho moved from the lighted kitchen into the shadowy

hall and then into the steamy room. The mirror was misted and there were no reflections. There was enough light from the kitchen to fill the bathroom with a soft gloaming.

"I had plenty of money – well, not plenty but enough," Angela said. "You didn't have to give me that ten dollars."

"I'd have only wasted it if I'd kept it," Tycho said. "I'd have spent it on a first-anniversary present for Africa. It sounds as if that would have been a dead loss."

"What's wrong with the world is this," Angela said, "that when you want to do something really dreadful, something terrible, almost all you can think of, off-hand, is getting drunk. It shows what a miserable little city we're in, doesn't it?"

"There must be worse things than that," Tycho said restlessly. "You just didn't know how to get to them."

"I thought of going around to my father's house and cutting his tennis net," Angela said. "But I wanted to do something really degraded. I mean, he's made me feel degraded in a way, and so I wanted to make it come true in all ways. I don't know why now. Just for a bit there, he made me hate myself, but I don't have to be his victim."

"I don't think I want to hear this story," Tycho said. Something occurred to him. "I'm going to ring your mother and let her know you're all right." He stood up.

"Don't you dare move," Angela cried. "Dido can wait for a few more minutes. Serve her right for feeding me up on that sickly story for years and years. Are you sitting down again?"

Tycho paused irresolutely.

"If you try to phone, I'll come out and stop you," Angela said. Tycho slowly sat down on the end of the bath.

"Are you sitting comfortably?" Angela asked him, bubbling a little bit because she was letting the water flow over her face.

"Yes, Miss," Tycho replied.

"Well, I went to Haydon's – that's supposed to be a really terrible place where the gangs hang out and fight and spit, and vomit on the floor. Well, there weren't many people there, but I got picked up straight off. This man came over and offered to buy me a drink, and I said, 'Thank you, I'll have a Fallen Angel.' "

"What?" Tycho asked. "What did you say you wanted?"

"It's a drink. I saw a picture of it in a book once. I thought you'd be pleased with me for thinking of such a symbolic thing, a simile or a metaphor or something."

"What sort of drink is it?" Tycho asked.

"A green one," Angela said. "It's got green stuff in it, and two dippers of gin."

"Dippers?" Tycho exclaimed.

"You know – they tip the bottle upside down twice – two measures. That's what I mean. I watched the barman make it. I had quite a lot of them – about five green metaphors."

"And they served you?" Tycho asked disapprovingly.

"Did they ever!" exclaimed Angela with enthusiasm. "They were pleased to have someone ordering such an expensive drink over and over again. You people aren't short of hot water are you?" She broke off with sudden anxiety.

"There's always plenty. Don't worry," Tycho said, half-thinking of a pun about being in hot water, and then deciding against it.

"We have to be so careful of water only having rainwater tanks," Angela cried. "This is wonderful bliss. Where was I? Oh yes – all set to ruin myself."

Tycho now understood very vividly what Angela's mother had meant when she had said that Angela might go up to the top of a cliff and then fall over by accident.

"I thought I'd do away with all this doubt and hope and stuff," Angela shouted. He could hear the sound of the shower, and the sound of water trickling off Angela. "Anyhow, I went staggering out with this guy to the disgust of all. We went down to the river bank... it's not a good time of year to be seduced in. It takes too long to get dark."

"I don't want to hear any more," Tycho called back, standing up. He heard the water turned off, and saw Angela's arm come out of the shower, silver with water and steam, saw her pick up the towel he had given her.

"You don't need to worry," Angela said, with a certain bitterness in her voice. "It worked, even though it was lies, I mean the idea of love and everything. I wasn't a child of love, but I might just as well have been. I couldn't bear to do without it in the end."

Tycho felt a moment of sympathy with the unknown man who had picked Angela up in the pub, bought her

Fallen Angels, staggered with her down to the river bank, and then found that she couldn't bear to do without love after all.

"He could!" Angela said. "I don't really blame him because I'd sort of led him on and I – oh well, he did try to insist, but first I was sick on him, and that's not very attractive, is it? I remember him shouting about his shoes and how much they cost, and I jumped right into the river down there by the old iron bridge – it's pretty shallow – and waded across to the other side."

Tycho saw her arm come out again.

"The river's full of broken glass," he said. "Lucky you didn't cut your feet to pieces." Angela didn't reply at once, and when she did it was to start another subject altogether.

"You wear old-fashioned underpants," she remarked. "Where do you get them from?"

Tycho was taken aback – shy. He wasn't sure if the steam had actually weakened him, or if he was just a little dizzy with relief because her story was an account rather than a confession.

"I couldn't do it!" Angela repeated. "So then I thought of Robin, and I decided I couldn't do that either. Mind you, just as well, because I don't think he'd have been very thrilled to have me turn up all smelly and disreputable. But I didn't think of that then. I sat there in the bushes feeling sorry for myself and, after a bit, I was sick again – terribly sick – and then I went to sleep for a bit. Really, I suppose I flaked out."

"When was this?" Tycho asked, watching his jersey

vanish into the shower. He felt he was watching a sort of striptease in reverse. He thought of her pulling his jersey, with something of his shape still in it, down over her head, and over her body as if she had pulled his hide down over hers.

"It was dark," Angela said doubtfully, "but just dark. I don't know. The shops were still open when I got back into town. I bought one thing – and had two cups of coffee, and then I walked here. It takes ages, but I didn't even have a bus fare left."

"How did you feel when you woke up again?" Tycho asked.

Angela stepped out of the shower alcove fully dressed in Tycho's clothes. "Not too bad, considering!" she said. "I think I'd been so sick that I was saved from too much of a hangover. I felt very shaky and I felt – I don't know – I felt so stupid! I felt silly. Never mind. It could have been a lot worse," she exclaimed irritably.

They went into the kitchen. There, in the full light, he saw her restored to herself, her red hair dark and wet, flattened against her head, her skin still pale and looking almost translucent, her eyes already almost back to normal.

"I was a bit defiled, I suppose," she said thoughtfully. "I was self-defiled but not very badly, even. I think it must take some practice to be really properly defiled. You can't do it all in one go. You have to do it in stages. Now I'm going to ask you the most intimate thing a woman can ask a man," she went on, standing over him. "Are you prepared? It's a request for the most private, possible thing in the world."

Tycho looked at his own jersey and remembered he had once hidden *The Joy of Sex* under it. "What do you want?" he asked her.

"Would you let me use your toothbrush?" she asked. "I wouldn't ask just anyone."

"Why not?" Tycho said. He went back to the bathroom to find his brush. "Just this once. But bring your own next time."

While Angela brushed her teeth he returned to the kitchen, poured out the coffee into two tall mugs and took the sandwiches out, beautifully toasted.

"Let's go and sit in with the Ionians," Angela said, looking at the supper with undisguised pleasure. "I don't mind the kitchen, except that whenever I'm here I can feel your mother disapproving of me in that smiling way she's got."

Tycho hesitated, and then carried the tray through into his bedroom. "I still don't know exactly what your father said to you," he said.

"Who? Oh him!" said Angela, setting her teeth. "Stuff him!" Then she looked at him and, after a moment, she began to tell him about her meeting with Roland Chase in a light, inconsequential voice that reminded him of Dido. When she told him about Roland's mother coming in and suddenly laying claim to the name of Angela with such disconcerting eagerness, she began to cry again, but with neither persistence nor passion. She sat on his bed, and Tycho sat on the seagrass matting at her feet.

"Can I tell you something?" she asked rather unnecessarily. "I mean something that..." She fell silent, looking at him uncertainly.

"Probably," Tycho said cautiously. "I don't think I'd be too shocked. I mean, I'm not hopelessly shocked so far."

"No one thinks I'm a virgin," Angela said. "But I still am. I mean I've gone pretty far at times but never... I still actually am."

Tycho stirred his coffee and looked down into it, as if he might read something in its galactic spiral.

"I don't know why!" Angela cried out, answering a comment he hadn't made. "I've never minded that people thought otherwise. In a funny way being a virgin – a closet virgin – made me feel powerful, as if I still had a lot of choice that no one knew about – had something left to bargain with, or to offer, or something in reserve. Other girls told about having affairs and going to bed with boys, but I never needed to because everyone always thought I knew everything anyway. You did, didn't you?"

The room was very quiet when she stopped talking and listened for his answer. Tycho stared down at the seagrass matting. Not one of the Ionians had a good answer for him to fall back on. He had nothing to say, but Angela persisted.

"You thought I slept with Robin, didn't you (I could tell) and Vaughan, and that other boy that went away to Auckland."

"Lawrence," Tycho said.

"Yes, Lawrence. Just for a moment I couldn't even remember. You thought I did it with them, didn't you?"

"It seemed likely..." Tycho said at last.

"But only *statistically* likely!" cried Angela, parodying his own voice. "Statistically likely, but *just... not true.*" She patted the top of his head at each separate word. "So there, Big Science! Why didn't you ask me! I'd have told you. I nearly did several times, and then I'd think, Oh well, to hell with him. Let him think what he likes. And somehow it's worse because you always think you look like the Hunchback of Notre Dame or something. Why don't you forget about appearance for a bit?"

"Really good advice," Tycho said sarcastically, "but just being good isn't always enough where advice is concerned, is it? I mean you couldn't forget your father, could you?"

"A father's different," Angela said. "Do you want that last sandwich?"

"No," said Tycho. "You have it."

"A father's fundamental," Angela said, taking the last sandwich with enthusiasm. "Not mine, I don't mean. The *idea* of a father is."

"Maybe," said Tycho, "but a face is too, and the idea of a face. It's the first part of you anyone really sees, and people look at you and decide about you from your face. I mean decide if you're worth knowing any more about. It's as simple as that – so simple it's scary. And everyone worries about their face, or tries to pretend it doesn't matter what they look like, though everything in the world proves that it does. It isn't *all* that matters," he added in a more subdued voice. "I know that, but it's one of the first things that matters. Suppose you'd been ordinary-looking. I mightn't have wanted to lend you my felt pens when we were five. It's that rough!"

Angela was silent, eating her sandwich. "You're nothing to write home about," she said at last, "but you're not so bad really, you know. What have you been doing this evening, anyway?"

"Mucking around," Tycho said, but then he began to tell about the telescope and the stars. He meant to go on and talk about Richard's phone call, but instead he talked about the moons of Jupiter and wondered aloud to Angela why Amalthea should be so red, why Io should be starred with volcanoes and crossed with sulphur plains, with cliffs and fault lines. It was restful to talk of strange, faraway worlds sitting there in the familiar room while part of his mind turned over the things Angela had said. He wondered uneasily about his father, about Africa, about Hudson who had gone home to his mother and then, unexpectedly, wondered about Dido.

"Here," he said quickly, "go and ring your mother while we remember. You'll need a lift home."

The words sounded strange for some reason, falling awkwardly between them. Tycho refused to meet her eyes.

"OK," Angela said, getting up. "She'll be worried, I suppose. But she deserves to worry a bit," she ended defiantly.

"It's after one in the morning," Tycho said.

"Not all that late for a Friday night," Angela answered. When she left the room Tycho stood up and unexpectedly studied himself in the mirror, something he had often done, but had not planned to do on this occasion. He saw a short, thickset young man with fine, silky, corn-coloured hair hanging down low on his forehead to conceal its babyish height and roundness, framing his face in a long version of a pudding-basin haircut. The eyes, which his mother had said were nice eyes, were dark blue, set off by lashes and eyebrows so fair that he had sometimes thought of darkening them, but had always been too ashamed to try it. Angela's footsteps bounded urgently down the passage. He turned to meet her as she came into his room and she paused, giving him a strange look which he was unable to account for. She was carrying both the squashy purple parcel she had brought with her and *The Catalogue of the Universe*.

"What did your mother say?" Tycho asked.

"I saw this on the table and I forgot about phoning her," Angela said. "Tycho – I spent your ten dollars, but I spent it on a present for you. Here."

Tycho opened the parcel. In it was Angela's plum-coloured morning T-shirt, slightly grubby, but now inscribed with words in new, glossy-white capital letters, THE IONIANS RULE!

Tycho looked at it, and thought he might be about to cry. He was devoutly glad he had always been too shy to darken his eyelashes, for mascara would certainly have run down on either side of his undistinguished nose.

"I'm sick of this," Angela said. "I don't know everything I feel, but I do know this. You mustn't ever want anyone but me, Big Science. If you look at any other girl I'll kill her."

She dropped *The Catalogue of the Universe* in front of her on the floor. It fell with the sound of a gun shot. "Chance favours the prepared mind," quoted Angela reading over his shoulder. "Stand on that."

"Stand on a book?" began Tycho. "Stand on nature read in truth and law?"

"Just do it," she said, fixing him with an implacable stare.

Tycho obeyed. His eyes were now on a level with her own and he looked into a face worked on by various passions. Then Angela put her arms around him and pressed herself against him. In spite of the clothes she was wearing, his own clothes, ill-fitting and thick, it was almost as if she had offered herself naked. Tycho put his arms around her and held her close, feeling he must certainly prop himself up until he got over the thrilling news now delivered to him from all his astonished frontiers. Angela's breath trembled in her throat and they kissed. The kiss over, they hugged each other furiously and Tycho buried his face in her shoulder.

"I always knew that was a good book," he mumbled. "From now on I'll take it with me wherever I go."

"Only if I'm there too," Angela said. She took a handful of his hair but her fingers hesitated, grew soft, and in the end she stroked it very gently.

"Put out the light," Tycho said. "If I turn around I might break the spell. And I'll never dare to get off the book ever again."

"You!" said Angela. "You never do get off it. Of all the people in the world, Big Science, you're the one who stands on *The Catalogue of the Universe* every minute of the day."

They kissed again, and touched each other.

"Put out the light," Tycho repeated. "You never know – I might be a merciless beast in the dark."

"Who cares?" Angela asked, but she leaned forward, reached over his shoulder and switched the light off. He could feel her breathing, and that she had begun laughing too. "OK, now you can strip the boyish clothes from my limbs and lay my beautiful white body bare!"

"I'll have a go," Tycho said. "If you want me to. Don't laugh at me," he begged, but began laughing himself, assaulted by an incredulous happiness.

"And you really love me for my mind, don't you?" Angela added, putting his hand under his own jersey on to her naked breast. "Not just my body. That's what you're supposed to say."

"What mind are you talking about?" Tycho muttered.

"What body's that?"

They kissed for the third time and fell together in Tycho's darkness.

13

A LEAP INTO THE ABYSS

In the early morning Tycho woke with Angela beside him. He had wakened with her ghost so many times that he felt almost familiar with her presence, but not with her breathing, for her face was close to his and they were breathing the same air. Midnight had rung on his mother's sugar-voiced clock. The phantoms of romance had twisted in their slow, acrobatic tumble, beginning to perform new tricks. His particular myth, that of the cloak of ugliness, had been turned inside out and had proved to have a magical lining. Yesterday he had been a faithful friend, and today he was a lover.

Darkness dissolved; through a net of birdsong, limitless light began to flow. "Tonic clonic!" said a bellbird in the flaxbush next door, and these clearly tolled notes named the sort of seizure that his father sometimes suffered from, when the world crashed in on him unimpeded, demanding more response than his father's particular injured brain could supply. He thought of his parents, but they were on Africa's shore, in another country with Richard to look after them, so he went to sleep again. Waking a little later he found

Angela awake too, looking at him intently as if she were expecting the answer to an important question and, along with this intensity, she wore an expression he had never seen before, something so shy and private it faded in the moment of being observed.

"Do you know what I forgot to do? " she said. Tycho knew at once.

"Ring!" he said between his teeth. "We forgot to ring your mother." Leaping from bed, he ran naked down a hall which had not seen a naked person since one notorious occasion, over a year ago, when Richard had jumped out and flashed at Mr Potter, getting his own back for a lecture on the scruffiness of his clothes. The phone rang in the cottage up on the hills, but there was no answer.

"There's no one there," Tycho said blankly, staring down at the phone as if it had betrayed him.

"Give me a go," said Angela imperiously. "She's got to be there at this hour in the morning. You probably dialled wrongly."

There was no answer when Angela rang either.

"I'd better get home," she said. "Can you give me a lift – no – blast! You haven't got the car."

"No buses either. Not till late. It's Saturday!" Tycho said, as, in the odd Eden of the Potter kitchen, he and Angela stared at each other.

"We've spent all night together," Angela pointed out, wonderingly. "I didn't exactly mean to do that. Oh well, too late now."

"Let's get dressed and I'll walk you home," Tycho suggested.

"All the way to the top of Dry Creek Road? You're on!" Angela said, but she didn't go looking for clothes straight away. She took a step forward and frowned critically.

"You could always rub a bit of gel through your hair when you wash it," she said thoughtfully, pushing it up off his forehead. "That would give it a bit more body."

"Gel!" exclaimed Tycho, taken aback.

"People use it to get those spiky styles," Angela told him. "It's easy to use."

"Can't I just stay the way I am?" he asked.

"No way!" Angela said energetically. "Well, I suppose I might just put up with the Christopher Robin hairstyle, but you'll have to sling out that vinyl jacket you wear. I'm telling you now: that definitely goes!"

"There's still a lot of wear in it," Tycho protested, but without real spirit.

"Someone else can have the benefit then," Angela replied. "Give it to some charity that's not too particular what it takes. Where do you get your hair done? I've never liked to ask but..."

"My mother cuts it," Tycho replied. Angela burst out laughing.

"That figures!" she said. "Gosh, you really need me."

"I know," Tycho said. "Much more than you need me."

Angela's smile faded. "It's not a contest," she said. "There's no first prize, is there?"

"I just feel so stupid," Tycho began. "I don't know what to say..."

"Say nothing," Angela answered quickly. "No describing or working out."

"But..." Tycho persisted. But she shook her head at him and then put her hand over his mouth. During the night she had suddenly cried easily and confidently against his shoulder as if they were lovers who had been reunited after many years. Once she had said, "Are you happy?" and when he replied that he was, she had laughed aloud in the dark.

"What are we going to do?" Tycho asked her.

"Meet each day as it comes, I suppose," Angela replied optimistically.

A series of faceless days immediately advanced on Tycho. A convention was taking place somewhere in his private market place, and the days came towards him all wearing name tags, Monday, Tuesday, Wednesday in suits and ties, Saturday in jeans, all holding anonymous presents in plain wrappers (quantums of energy, romantic occasions), some prepared to kiss him, others wanting to take him by the throat.

"Well, if I give up my vinyl jacket will you stop wearing shirts people can see through?" he asked her.

"The vinyl jacket is non-negotiable," Angela said, looking a little taken aback. "Anyhow, I'm just trying to improve you, but you're just being possessive. I'm the noble one of us, this time." Then she hugged him overwhelmingly. "This is a bear-hug," she said, and pretended to growl in his ear. And then she looked in the fridge and complained because there was no fruit juice. Tycho tried ringing Dido again and made a pot of tea in the new teapot.

"We'll have to tidy up a bit," he said, "because my parents could come home while we're out and find two mugs, strange damp towels and everything."

"Are you ashamed?" Angela asked him, dressed in his own clothes again, but with a shirt instead of a jersey. "Would your mother have a fit if I left a pair of knickers under your pillow?" Then she remembered that she shouldn't talk lightly about fits in Tycho's family. "I'm sorry!" she said.

"They've got a lot of things to worry about," Tycho said, "But, apart from that, she'd have a lot to say that I don't much want to hear. Never mind. We'll worry about your mother first. I promised to ring her."

"But I put everything out of your head, didn't I?" said Angela, looking pleased.

They left the house, hiding the key under the loose stone at the corner of the porch, and began walking along the silent streets. The morning was fresh and marvellous, rooftops standing out sharply against the sky, lawns and footpaths and trees inhabited by birds. Iridescent starlings walked away from them in a rapid, ungainly fashion, blackbirds hopped across lawns in quick staccato lines... Tycho, reminded unexpectedly of sewing machines, half-expected to see a row of stitches behind them. Sparrows skirmished in the gutters, some of them followed by demanding young, quite as big as their parents.

They passed Centaurus Road School, where Dido had cleaned handbasins, lavatories, and had guided the eager, roaring, floor polisher. From the playground one could look up at the hills and see the dry creek and the bridge over it and the dark patch of trees that hid Angela's house. Angela looked up and saw her home in the air above her. And over there in that particular room, Tycho on his first day at school had tried to engage Angela's interest by lending her his felt pens. He wished there were some way he could reach back to his five-year-old self, optimistically looking forward to school and learning to read, still confident he was naturally lovable, and tell him, "Don't worry too much! It turns out all right." But there was no way it could be done. He had had to live, would always have to live through everything to reach this morning, and now he had reached it he couldn't simply stop there and enjoy it. Perhaps somewhere ahead a future self was walking past the school, wanting to reach him at this very moment in order to warn him.

Tycho stopped and made Angela stop too, and kissed her and made her kiss him back, for he did not want to hear any warning telling him not to be too happy.

"It's worse for you," Angela said, "because it says in the books that men are most sexy at about your age, but I've got to wait until I'm about forty. Does that count as more wobbling?"

"Did I tell you things wobbled?" Tycho asked her. "I must have been mad. Look!" He pranced along at the edge of the gutter. "Straight as an arrow. No hands!"

"Boast! Boast!" Angela said laughing, thrilled with his happiness.

They came to the corner shop, its usual notices and promises of ice creams and pies taken in for the night, blinds down, so that it presented a blank, unfamiliar face to the street.

Angela took his hand, but then decided to put her arm around his shoulders.

"It's good you're so short," she said. "My arm fits over your shoulder really well."

"But what if I have to carry you up the great staircase?" Tycho asked.

"I'll carry *you*, that's all," Angela replied. "I nearly had to, anyway."

"That's getting close to describing," Tycho said. "If I'm not allowed to describe, you aren't either. Your rules."

"Good rules, too," Angela said, "but more for you than me. What I thnk is this – I try to be modest, and then I end up secretly thinking I'm pretty good. But it works the other way round with you. You need to be protected from it."

"From what?" Tycho asked.

"Trying to work out what you're really and truly like," said Angela. "You always come up with a bad answer when you don't have to. "

They were walking among houses that were perhaps forty years old, the same age as the one Tycho lived in. However, as they climbed they entered a better neighbourhood, where the houses were built to command striking views of the city. Height and beauty had to be paid for. Tycho thought how strange it was that there was a narrow ribbon winding in and out over the hills that was somehow considered the best place to live. If people could not afford to live on the hills, they lived in streets like his own street – respectable, but cramped and homely. Yet to live on the very top of the hill, like Angela, was something different again. It suggested a family even poorer than his own, but free of the rules that restricted all the houses further down. Angela's house might have its lavatory tied to it by a brick path, but up there, water meant something different from what it meant further down, air meant something different, both wrestling with gravity as with an invisible angel.

"Lovely morning!" said the first man of the day, washing his car on the side of the road.

"Terrific," Tycho agreed, stepping over the little streams of water and detergent that flowed off the car.

"Good to be alive," the man said. It was just a jolly remark to a stranger, but it worried Angela.

"I don't know how I forgot to ring Dido," she said. "I was really sorry for what I said and particularly when she was feeling superstitious, too."

"She's not superstitious, is she?" Tycho asked, surprised.

"Not really," Angela said, "but there is something about living up there that makes you almost superstitious. No, that's not quite right. It's tooth-and-claw country in a way. Going up and down turns into a sort of test. It's like pitting your wits against the road. Sometimes you can't help thinking you might lose. You have to drive humbly, but not everyone does, of course."

"We'll be there in another twenty minutes," Tycho said.

"It'll take longer than that," Angela replied. "I know this road just so well. It hisses along," she said, tracing a great 'S' in the air with her finger, "and it gets even steeper around the next corner. When I was little I walked up here day after day." She trudged on a little ahead of him, speaking with a sort of proud nostalgia. "I used to have favourite friendly corners, and enemy ones. Some rocks and stones were kind and others were dangerous, lifting their eyes up out of the ground like crocodiles..." She broke off and stopped walking. "Tyke – I didn't want to go home defeated. Suppose you get a bit of a knock. Well, you just have to pick yourself up and go on to the next thing, don't you? Dido was right about leaving Roland Chase alone, but I had to make good come out of it if I could, somehow, didn't I? I couldn't just let myself be so wrong and have it come to nothing."

"I don't know if your mother's going to think going to bed with me is making good come out of anything," Tycho said.

"I didn't quite plan to do it," Angela said, looking puzzled. "Not like I planned to be degraded." She touched a letterbox and said, "Isn't it spooky to think the land is laid out in possible houses from now on up. It's haunted by numbers between two hundred and seventy-five and a thousand. It's all set down in the Land and Survey Office."

Tycho had worried about Dido, but found he could worry no more. He was filled with a happiness that crowded everything else out and, though he had always been a man of the universe, he now became a man of the world as well, astonished as every bend of the road carried him on up into a flowery countryside he could never have really noticed before, for the hills looked barren from the city. Only now he was actually walking on the road could he see the clovers and the yarrow, the bright, pure yellow of the flowering broom and the occasional purple of foxgloves. Sorrel was coming into bloom, shaking out flowers like grains of scarlet, and elderberry trees turned pale umbels towards him. His legs ached as the climb grew steeper and steeper again.

They turned a corner and, looking up, saw the long scar of the dry creek tumbling down into a deep cleft in the hills. Their road swept sideways into the same cleft, then back out along the opposite spur, bent itself around a rocky outcrop and came almost at once on to the bridge which straddled the groove cut into the land by the rushing water of other seasons.

"It's like the beginning of a helix," Tycho mumbled, looking at the elliptical rising curve of the road they must follow.

"Do you know what I said to her?" Angela asked Tycho uneasily.

"No, but you've had lots of quarrels with Dido," Tycho replied. "You've run away from home before. She might be mad at you, but you'll get over it."

"I said something fierce," Angela said. "But then I wanted to take the worst of it back directly I said it. What's that word that means you're defenceless?"

Tycho thought for a moment, climbing on.

"Vulnerable," he suggested after a moment, but he was never to know if he were right or wrong.

"There she is! What on earth is she doing?" Angela suddenly cried in relief and surprise, and around the far corner came a cloud of dust with a streak of blue in its heart.

"Mind you, she's got to apologise, too," Angela said quickly. The car rattled on to the bridge, and scattered the gravel as it came off again. It did not try to turn, simply going straight ahead. Then it plunged right through the narrow border of unfurling bracken, golden fronds rising above the purplish brown of last year's growth, plunged straight through the worst fence in the world and flew off effortlessly into the space beyond. For a point of time it seemed to hang in the clear air, almost as if it were choosing whether to go on or back again. But it fell, turning as it fell. They heard it strike the slope below, and a moment later the horrible crash of metal, bruising and mangling, came to their ears.

Angela gave a cry such as Tycho had never heard before, a cry so remarkable it froze him. He had barely had time to record the fact of the car's fall before this inhuman voice sounded beside him. She made for the place where the fence sagged away from the edge of the road, repeated her cry, leapt and vanished, leaving Tycho alone with hills, sky, flowers and a silence rushing in to heal the air, a silence so deep and powerful it felt terminal, like a silence that would never be broken again.

14

THE DRAGON'S CAVE

Angela's leap carried her down perhaps ten feet, over an abrupt bank, to crash among grass and broom and crocodile rocks, but though she tumbled forward on to her knees she was not hurt. Within a moment she was slipping and sliding down into the cleft, not looking back once at Tycho who was following more cautiously.

By running down one side of the cleft and up the other side one might indeed reach in the shortest possible time that smashed blue toy which had not fallen very far down the slope in spite of its prodigious leap.

It lay on its back lodged on an outcrop of rock, half-concealed by vertical scribbles of tough green broom bushes pushing in close around it. Whole minutes of scrambling separated them from the car but they were divided from it by so little space they could see its helpless wheels turning at right angles to the spin of the world. They could even see, between broom and elderberry bushes, a foxglove forest, rank on rank of tall flowers, all looking east, all looking down, as if at the sound of the crash they had swivelled their long giraffe-necks within their collars of green leaves and were waiting to witness a miracle.

Angela fell again, stumbling in silence and rolling over and over as if she had entered a state in which the only direction was forward, in which up and down had ceased to matter. Once again she regained her feet and ran on in a silence eerie in a person normally prepared to rage and curse at opposition. But the savage sound that had accompanied her leap had carried her back into a state before language. There were no words or sounds left to her as she flung out her arms, looking as if she were about to fly out across the cleft, but really compensating for the slope, forcing a balance, a symmetry all her own, out of the pitching world.

As for Tycho, his whole life already transformed, was transformed yet again by the fiery spirit who had wept on his shoulder only a few hours ago, who had laughed with joy because she had the power to make him happy. She fled burning before him, her hair a nimbus of living fire as the sun, spinning up from the east like a wheel of gold, touched it into life – a being more directly composed of earth, fire and water, Tycho thought, than anyone else he knew.

They reached the bottom of the cleft at the place where the groove of the dry creek ran into it, crossed themselves with a rattle and a rustle, stumbling over stones and a few scripts and scrolls of the bark shed by the native fuschia. Then, scrambling like monkeys, they pulled themselves up the opposite slope, clutching handful after handful of the earth's hair. They were both so intent on their climb that it came as a great shock when a man shouted at them, a shout without words, desperate enough but still human, in no way resembling Angela's primal shriek as she tried to fly but could only fall. Angela stopped as if she had struck a wall.

"It's the Cherrys!" she exclaimed, in a wheezing voice, blown out on a wild breath. "Of course, it's the Cherrys."

The voice shouted again, even more urgently.

"All the same – come on!" Tycho gasped, but now he went ahead, as Angela, her most personal fear gone, lost something of the power that enabled her to plunge down one hillside and a third of the way up another like a demented genie. Now she had only her normal speed and strength, and felt weariness just as Tycho did.

"I just couldn't see," she cried behind him, but Tycho made no reply. As she had found speech, he had lost it.

Phil Cherry, yellow with pain and shock and fear, was sitting among the foxgloves, cradling his right arm as if he were nursing a baby.

"For God's sake!" he cried. "Get Jerry out. He's still in there."

Tycho thought he should not consider what he might find in the car which, its remoteness gone, had all the horror of fresh ruin. One side had compacted so that it looked like a sardine can which someone had tried to open with a brutal hammer. The other side bulged towards them, snarling with glassy teeth, one door hanging by a single hinge across the narrow space of its doorway, which has half as tall as it should be. Beyond the door, set in this twisted frame, he could see a human arm, the hand limp as Adam's before it was touched into life by God. Tycho did not slacken his step, though. Quick as the shadow of the eclipsing moon, he was attacked by the thought that he would seize the arm, pull it towards him and find there was no man attached. He was struck by a smell that reminded him of the fires that burn perpetually on rubbish dumps and, more chillingly, the sharp smell – chemical, dangerous and somehow fascinating – of petrol still pumping from an artery somewhere inside the mangled iron guts of the car – a car that had become both a fatally injured animal and a tortured extension of the hillside – an outcrop of iron, a dark cave with a dragon in it, preparing to roar.

"Tyke. Please!" Angela called after him. "Tyke, it's too late. You'll be killed." Though she was so close behind him, she was in as much danger as he. The southerly wind swept down the slope from behind them and smoke streamed away from the car, visibly darkening as it grew more confident, a spirit departing as the car died.

"Are you there?" Tycho cried, crawling on his hands and knees at the door of the cave, paying a social call on the smouldering dragon, who, as the gust of wind died, suddenly filled the car with a thick smoke of a kind Tycho had never seen before, so dense and black he felt he could have grabbed handfuls of it. As he felt its stinking breath strike his face, Tycho, half in the car, felt for the arm, seized it and pulled. So far from coming easily, it resisted him, sluggish and heavy in his hands. Someone beyond the smoke coughed and choked, and Tycho, bracing his feet on the edge of the car, tugged wildly and roughly, felt something yield, tried to breathe, then coughed and choked himself. Someone flung arms around his waist and pulled with him, and reluctantly the dragon began to surrender its prey, not being quite powerful enough to hold it back. But the southerly breeze blew again, pushing the smoke out to the northeast, yet also encouraging the dragon, for somewhere in the black fog there was a sound rather like hollow hands clapping together. A wall of unbearable heat swept towards Tycho, so that he screamed aloud as Angela and he tugged Jerry Cherry, a huge bleeding doll, clear of the cave. And then the dragon really began to roar.

Scampering, like two children playing with a third, Angela and Tycho retreated back among the foxgloves, dragging Jerry Cherry after them, and leaving red smears over the green and gold wires and blades of the grass. Each moment before the dragon's cave had seemed an hour, but their rescue had only taken a few seconds. And now the dragon raved furiously. The heat and smell were like solid presences, the smoke, heavy and dirty, went rolling out over the slope below, over further wild flowers and grasses, and foxglove forests, out to the wedge of the city driven in between the hills.

"It'll explode," Angela yelled.

"Explode! What do you think this is? Bloody television?" cried Phil. But he was wrong, for the car began a series of explosions, popping and banging as they struggled still further away from it, Jerry unconscious and silent, Phil swearing and sweating with pain.

"Is he OK?" he cried. "Is Jerry OK?"

"I don't know!" Tycho said, pausing to look at what he had rescued. "Oh! Oh no, he's not! Something terrible's happened to his legs."

"He's alive," Angela said. "He's bleeding. How do we stop it though? He'll bleed to death."

"I don't know," Tycho said, pulling off the T-shirt, Angela's present from last night. "Just hold something against the bleeding." To himself he was thinking, all for nothing! There's too much wrong! There's too much happening and none of us knows what to do.

"We need the ambulance," Angela cried. "Ours must be the nearest phone." Both she and Jerry looked up towards the place where 1000 Dry Creek Road lurked in its guardian trees.

"Miles!" Phil said, simply meaning it was a long way off.

"I'll go, though." Angela stood up. "I'll be as fast as I can."

"Hang on a moment," said Tycho. "I can hear a car. We might be able to flag it down. It can't miss the smoke."

Blood made his hands slippery, and darkened the word IONIANS as he tried to staunch the blood that ran so richly from Jerry Cherry. Beyond them the fire burned on as the dragon ate everything it could find. There was another explosion.

"That'll be the battery," Phil said.

Over the car the tormented air shivered and twisted. To

Angela, at least, it seemed they were in the presence of a mirage, a wild phantom event welded into the rest of reality by uneasy seams that might yield at any moment, carrying the burning car and the bleeding man out of their dimension, leaving them on the hillside pinned between the downward gaze of the foxgloves and the upward glance of the city, thrusting itself deep into a cleft in the hillside, far below them.

The car they had heard was coming in the opposite direction from the one Tycho had expected. It was coming down the hill from above them. It came round the corner, drove slowly over the bridge and drew off the road at the bend beyond. Someone climbed out and stood for just a moment looking down on them. It was Dido.

15

THREE-MINUTE HERO

Dido came down the hillside with a steady crab-like movement, halfway between jumping and striding, leaping on to her left leg, bringing her right down beside it, and leaping again. Her dark brown hair, streaked with grey and with lighter strands bleached by sun and hot northwest winds, hung down in long, snaky locks which flew up around her with each step. She wore a straight green dress, rather too long for her, and Angela's old kicked-around school shoes, and looked like the wise woman of the hills come out of a hole in the ground to rescue lost travellers.

"Dido," Angela shouted up to her. "Dido! I thought it was you in that car!"

Dido appeared to cover the last few yards in a single bound. Tycho, glancing up, thought she was flying down on them. Her hand went out to Angela, though she did not look directly at her for more than a second. They held hands briefly.

"I heard the noise!" she said. "When I realised there had been a crash I thought it might be you!" She grimaced over Jerry's condition.

"He's breathing, anyway," she said.

"I checked that," Tycho said. "We just yanked him out. We probably killed him, but..."

He did not need to say anything more. Beyond them the car still burned and cracked the air around it like a whip. The broom bushes near it blackened and crackled. Dido kneeled beside him.

"There's an ambulance on the way," she said, and looked over at Phil. "Phil – are you all right?" sounding astonished, and Phil gave a brief, wincing grin.

"I fell out!" he said – in a more friendly voice than any Angela had heard from him before. "We weren't wearing seat belts. Well, I mean to say, we were just running down the road... someone had said there were a few sheep out again." But Dido and Angela knew the Cherrys regarded the roadside as part of their proper grazing ground. Tycho thought that if Jerry had been wearing a seat belt he would not have been flung round, but then it would also have been impossible to have dragged him out.

"I reckon I've broke my shoulder," Phil said. He swore rather badly, describing how much it hurt, and in the same breath, looking at Jerry, said with unmistakable grief, "Oh gawd, look at him. He's a gonner."

"These cuts on his face must be from flying glass," Dido said. "And he might have had a bang there on the side of the head, but I can't do anything about that."

"Should we try putting a tourniquet on his leg?" Tycho asked doubtfully, and Dido said, equally doubtfully, "No, I don't think they do that now. Just keep on holding something against the worst places. Here – I'll take over."

"I will," Angela offered eagerly, but she was shivering and hugging herself to stop her own trembling. "I thought it was you!" she repeated, tears running down her face, and her bottom lip trembling.

"Here, see if you can't get my shirt off," Phil said. "I can't get it off myself. Cut it off. I've got a knife on my belt."

Angela took Phil's knife and stood dangerously over him. Tycho passed his sodden T-shirt to Dido and shook his hands to get his own trembling out of them. Somewhere, in the quiet, early morning, he could hear the warble of magpies, and then, very far away, a whooping, wailing insect voice singing a familiar city song.

"That might be the ambulance," Tycho said. "Did you just ring one on a hunch?"

"Someone saw it happen," Dido answered, clamping her hand against the bloody lacerations around Jerry's feet and legs. He had immensely strong-looking, muscular thighs, handsomely set off by his work shorts. One foot wore the remains of a sandal.

"Old Mrs Hansen down by the school rang," Dido continued. "I was on the verandah and I heard the crash, and while I was still wondering what it was, and where it came from, and whether to investigate, the phone rang." The voice of the siren seemed to have stopped. Dido hesitated in her story, apparently listening for it. "It was Mrs Hansen saying a car had gone over at Dry Creek bridge. She knew I was the closest person to whatever accident there had been."

"We rang you earlier," Angela said, "but you weren't there." She had half-cut and half-torn Phil's faded work shirt from him.

"I listened for the phone all night," Dido said. "Then I got so sick of the house and the phone not ringing I went for a walk right over the top of the hill and looked at the sea."

The city and the bottom of the cleft were now blotted out by thick, black, evil-smelling smoke. Just at the edge, where it thinned out, however, Tycho could make out the school playground a long, long way below. He tried to imagine himself there, looking up.

"I told him to take it easy," Phil said. "I said, 'Slow down over the bridge!' We both knew the brakes were a bit Mickey-Mouse."

"Where's that damned ambulance?" Dido looked around, showing signs of anxiety for the first time, but as she spoke, its siren burst out again. Some turn in the road or thrust of the hill had masked it for a while. It came closer and closer, still wailing a song, part warning and part lament. Angela gave her mother part of the torn shirt to hold against Phil's wounds.

"He dabbed the brakes," Phil was explaining. "Nothing happened! Then he jammed his foot down to the boards, but hell – there was absolutely nothing there. We were over the edge in a flash."

"You jumped off. You didn't just topple," Angela said.

"There was nothing there," Phil repeated defensively.

"Did that old lady who lives on the far side of the school ring?" Tycho asked. He could scarcely believe it. "Her house must be about a thousand feet down."

"She has her grand-daughter staying with her (Tycho, could you take over here for a moment while I wipe my hands) – and she was up earlier showing her the hens and the view of the dry creek bed. You can see it from down there. 'Look,' she said. 'There goes a car – just like a doll's-house car.' And the next moment they both saw it go over. Mrs Hansen wasn't too sure what she'd seen, but the girl was. They phoned the ambulance, and then she remembered me stuck away up there and she phoned me too. She remembers me from my school-cleaning days."

"She used to babysit for me after school," Angela said.

The ambulance wailed overhead. The familiar white van appeared and, at last, parked nose to nose with Dido's car. Two men were out in an instant and moving down towards them almost without hesitation, as an incoherent sound made itself heard. Jerry groaned strangely, eyes still closed, sounding to Tycho not so much like a man whose legs were shattered and torn as someone whose heart was broken.

A moment later the two ambulance men were with them. The crisis had become somebody else's routine. Another strange voice was heard as the two men spoke with a third up in the van through their portable radio.

"I checked he was breathing," Tycho said.

"Good lad," said the first ambulance man.

"Are there only the two of you?" Dido asked. "It seems such a difficult place to get anyone out of."

"The senior station officer's up in the van," said the second man. "We can bring in another ambulance if we need to."

"I want to go home," Angela said to her mother. "I really, really thought it was you. It made something go wrong with my eyes. Mostly I know the car from miles off."

She was weeping rather like a person who can't hold any more and has to overflow, with no particular fuss – simply a constant fall of tears.

"I don't think we can do any more good here," Dido said. "We'll only be in the way. We're the nearest phone. Should we ring the police or anything?"

"All done," said the first man briefly. "We alert them immediately. They could be along any time, depending on how busy they are."

"I didn't see the accident," Dido said. "My daughter did, but we're easy to find if they want to ask us anything."

"The brakes failed," Phil was insisting somewhere. "I told Jerry to get them seen to, but he reckoned he could drive anything on wheels, with or without brakes, and drive the crate it came in, too."

Dido took Angela's hand. Angela looked over at Tycho.

"See you around, Big Science!" she said. "I'll ring you."

To Tycho this sounded like the sort of thing employers were supposed to say if they didn't want to employ you.

"See you!" he said, lifting his hand in an uncertain gesture that was not quite a wave. He watched them begin to climb up to their car, leaving him, holding his sodden T-shirt. If you looked closely the Ionians still ruled on it, but less confidently than they had first thing in the morning, when it seemed he had achieved a predictable ending to his fairy tale.

"I would rather understand one cause than be the King of Persia," Democritus had once said. Tycho looked over at the ambulance man, busy with Jerry, watched the sullen black smoke drifting sluggishly away from the car, looked up to watch Dido and Angela preparing to drive away. "How did I get here?" he wondered, trying to work out just why he was there on a hillside simultaneously beautiful and horrible. He could name causes, but it seemed he couldn't understand one of them. The Ionians had been experimental men (according to Carl Sagan who had spoken about them on television) who had tried to reason their way in beyond superstition had tried uniting practical skills with those of the imagination, and to govern what was governable by understanding it.

Anaximander of Miletus had done one of the first recorded experiments with a stick and a shadow, had accurately determined the length of the year and the time of each season. But who could determine the sort of seasons Tycho lived with, where spring could yield so suddenly to a season that was neither summer, autumn nor winter. In this fifth season, for which he had no name, he could sit, a saviour of some kind, yet coloured like a butcher, watching Angela go away from him without once looking back.

"See you around, Big Science!" she had said, but what more could she have said, at that place, at that time?

On the road above there was a scatter of gravel. A breakdown truck arrived and parked like a sort of vulture waiting for the car to die. A man got out and began talking to the senior station officer in the ambulance. Tycho couldn't imagine the car would ever be of any use to anyone in any form ever again.

"You can't tell me they weren't listening in," mumbled one ambulance man to his companion.

"No rule against listening in," said the other, "provided nobody acts on what they hear. You wait though! He'll say he got tipped off by somebody."

The police car arrived; the injured men were being taken up the hillside. The breakdown-truck man came down and was helpful with ropes and the stretcher.

"Nothing for us this time," Tycho heard him say. "It's burnt out, and that chassis must be shot to bits after a prang like that."

There was no mercy for Tycho. Thought after thought crowded in on him, some only half-finished. They jostled to find a place of power in his consciousness as if every mind in the world but his was dying and he was the sole, safe repository of understanding. Once in him, they bred like miraculous but threatening viruses, turning their faces towards him, as the foxgloves had done. It would take a long time to understand what he was producing, or absorbing, in such ferociously concentrated bursts.

Yesterday he could have watched Angela walk off with Robin and felt mainly resignation, but the view for a man standing on *The Catalogue of the Universe* was different and, once standing there, you couldn't just step off again. The book was only an inch or two thick, but the fall was infinite. Now he found he was hoping, as rashly as he had hoped in childhood, that someone would love him better than anything else in the world, though not being a child any more, he could no longer believe he was naturally good or wise, or had any of the qualities that should ensure love. After all, it was given out according to non-predictable and therefore non-Ionian principles. The Ionians lived, but other things lived along with them. For all that, the very fact that love wobbled so violently in its unstable orbit was the source of his new hope that, in spite of everything, he might be allowed to give and receive it beyond a single hour.

He pulled his way up towards the ambulance in the wake of more efficient men.

("Very nice sir! Lovely fit!" said a mysterious tailor in his private market-place, pinning him up in some new hopes. "Now we'll run up some nice new fears. They'll set it off a treat." "Oh I don't think I'll bother with the fears," said Tycho nervously. "Sir, you can't really have one without the other," the tailor said. "Not a gentleman of your style, if you don't mind me saying so. They're co-ordinated.")

"Are you all right?" asked someone beside him. "You weren't in the car, were you? You're the young fellow who pulled the injured man out."

"I'm all right really," Tycho said. "My hands hurt." He had nearly said that he had been watching too many television advertisements, because real life was beginning to seem like television. The officer led him to the ambulance where Jerry was strapped in a bunk.

"We've got to get him to casualty immediately," said one of the men. "Hop in, and we'll take you in, too. His face is slightly burned, so it's a fair bet that when the fire first really blazed up you copped it too. You took a bit of a chance, didn't you?"

"It went up with a sort of 'whoof!'" Tycho said. "There was a little bit of smoke and suddenly all that stinking black stuff." He could smell it still.

"It's the polyurethane," someone said.

"Could I just have your name and address?" asked the officer.

Somewhere behind Tycho someone else said, talking of Jerry, "Poor bastard! It's not just the injuries, it's the shock."

The ambulance moved. It swung around in the road in three deft movements.

"You've lost your eyebrows, I'd say," one of the ambulance men remarked to Tycho, "and a bit of your front hair."

"I've never been very strong on eyebrows," Tycho said, "and some people say my hair looks like Christopher Robin's. Actually I was trying to copy Carl Sagan."

It was quite a long time before Tycho found himself in his own street once more. He arrived home, wearing a strange black jacket shot through with lurex stripes, something that had apparently been left at the hospital by some other casualty over a year ago.

"I'll drop it back," Tycho had promised.

"Do me a favour, love, and keep it," the woman in the office had said to him. "It's been there ages. It's sunny out, but there's a bit of an easterly. You might be glad of it."

Tycho carried his T-shirt in a plastic bag. He had enough money to get a bus to the city square, and then to catch another one that stopped only a few yards from his house.

"Sure you're all right?" the staff nurse asked him. Tycho thought this was very kind of her for she was busy, and though his burns were very painful they were not severe. After a long wait in the square, for as it was Saturday morning the buses were infrequent, he approached his home, feeling, as Angela had felt coming out of her father's office the day before, that everything had changed. It was like coming home after an absence of years. His home gate seemed luminous with significance – unreal, yet entirely familiar.

There was a tiny child just inside the gate, carefully pulling himself on to his feet, for he could not stand alone. His feet looked too small and fat and pink to hold a human being erect, but he rose up to look at the world, and at Tycho, through the bars of the gate. He was pleased to be upright, and beamed so widely at Tycho through the bars that he dribbled a little bit. A dew drop hung from his chin and his new teeth shone in the middle of his smile. Everything about this boy, eyebrows and all, was fresh.

Tycho knew him well. It was his nephew, Hamish, so that meant Africa must be home. Tycho felt neither dismay nor pleasure, for he had very few feelings left to lavish on anything. He opened the gate carefully, shut it, making sure the latch clicked so that no crawling nephew could escape out into the world before he could manage it, and picked Hamish up, anyway, just to make sure. As he carried him up the drive he smelled baby powder and tinned baby food, while Hamish looked curiously back at him, probably smelling the hospital smell, and maybe the smell of the burning car still clinging around his hair. As they walked around the corner of the house, Richard came out looking distracted, dressed in a Russian blouse, leather trousers patched on the knees and a slightly moth-eaten fur bolero he had discovered on the white-elephant stall of a church fair. Richard looked tired, distracted and unexpectedly subdued.

"Aren't you too hot?" Tycho asked, looking at his brother's clothes, but Richard was only interested in Hamish.

"Oh *there* he is, poor kid! I was sent out to look for him. Kitchy koo, Hamish!" he said in a kind, but disinterested voice, and went on without a pause. "My God, we've just had the most incredible twenty-four hours. You wouldn't believe it."

Tycho carried Hamish in across the verandah and into the kitchen. A comfortable chair had been brought into the kitchen for his father to sit in, and Africa and his mother confronted each other across the table, as if they were about to begin some sort of arm wrestling. Tycho stood in the doorway and saw them, held still for a moment by his entrance, in a living family portrait.

"Hello, Tyke," Africa said. "You see, the bad penny's come home again. Richard said you predicted this."

"Oh dear," said Mrs Potter. "Tyke doesn't understand anything. He doesn't realise how complicated life can be, and you don't either. You've only been married a year, and what's a year out of a whole lifetime. You have to give things a real chance."

"I did predict it, but not so soon," Tycho replied, with a faint grin which, after a moment, Africa returned. "Anyhow, I suppose there's nothing to say you won't go back again."

"There's *me* to say it!" Africa exclaimed.

"We shouldn't give in to failure," Mr Potter declared. "I've no doubt Hudson can be very irritating – well, I find him irritating myself, I'll admit that now, but..."

"I don't mind admitting failure," Africa cried. "Why not? Face up to it, and it sets you free to do better. I'll go back, but only to collect a few things, my share of the wedding presents for example – and that's all."

"Africa, you sound so hard," mourned Mrs Potter.

A suitcase lay half-unpacked in the middle of the kitchen floor, with packets of disposable nappies piled beside it. Tycho jiggled Hamish a little bit, as much to entertain himself as the baby, and wondered if he had ever looked as wonderfully fresh, with such round cheeks and exquisitely clear eyes.

"Little Ham!" he said, holding him tightly because he felt

sorry for him, even though Hamish was still pleased with himself and everything around him.

"And what have you been up to?" his father asked suddenly. "Where did you get that revolting jacket?"

"Yeah, man!" said Richard promptly. "Where did you get the threads, man?"

"Don't use that jargon in this house," Mr Potter said, more from habit than because he was seriously annoyed. "Tycho – you look a mess. What have you done to the front of your hair?"

"I went to this place – it's the latest thing," Tycho said. "They singe your hair off with a blowlamp. It seals the end of the hair and your vital essence doesn't leak away."

"It suits you," Richard said. "I love the frizzly bits. What have you really been up to?"

"It's a long story," Tycho said. "I'll tidy up, though, before I tell you." He put Hamish down and went to his room. He could smell the smell of burning car following him like a ghost. Even cleaned up, his face looked wild and strange, the forehead flushed as if with sunburn, one eyebrow more insignificant than the other. As he tidied himself up as best he could, Richard came in, tossed the ironing on to the floor, and flung himself down on the other bed, spare no longer, staring at the ceiling.

"Why is this particular bit of the ceiling so familiar?" he asked. "Can I have seen it before in another life?" His voice changed. "She really *is* home, you know."

"I didn't like to ask in front of Dad and Mum, but is

Hudson – you know – playing around?" Tycho asked delicately.

"Hudson? Do me a favour!" said Richard. "*She* is! Africa! She's fallen in love with some academic who lectures in that university extension course that's supposed to prevent young married women from turning into mindless cabbages." After "middle class", "academic" was Richard's strongest term of abuse.

"You've got to be joking!" Tycho exclaimed, genuinely astonished.

"Scouts' honour!" Richard said, giving the scout salute and making it look rather rude. "Much more *our* sort of person," he said, mimicking his mother's voice, "not like that poor peasant, Hudson. Not that Mum approves. Oh well – there was the most awful fight last night, just before I rang you. Apparently while the party, such as it was, was at its chilly height, which was only about, oh *so* high," said Richard, turning over on his bed and holding his hand about half an inch from the floor, "the lecturer, overcome by concern or lust or something, rang her, and Hudson answered the phone and recognised this unexpectedly cultured voice, and then the fun really started."

"I'll bet," Tycho said.

"There was Hudson, pettishly flinging his toothbrush and what he could find of his pyjamas into a suitcase, and his mother carrying him off – and poor Dad had a bad turn – not because of the fuss, I think, just because he's apparently been trying to get himself off the drugs ("Phasing it out," he called it) without any medical permission, *and* he'd had a drink or two or three. And then Africa phoned the lecturer, and he came around in his car, but she wouldn't bring him in. She went and sat out in the car with him, and I dropped off into a light, refreshing doze (on the floor because she was having the settee) and then she came in about half-past three, and stood on my face in the dark. It was that sort of night."

"Some poor people probably long for a night like that," Tycho said. "People with nothing to do but watch telly."

"And first thing this morning Hudson was on the phone telling Africa that Hamish was his son, too, and he'd probably get custody," Richard went on. "I suppose he might. He's really fond of him. So's Hudson's mother. It's going to be a great war of the grannies."

"Is Africa still feeding him?" Tycho asked. "Wasn't he going to be brought up entirely naturally until he was forty-six, or something?"

Richard did not know. "The lecturer's name is Morris," he said. "Timothy Morris. Doesn't that sound chaste. I said he wouldn't do. We've got one Morris already – Morris-the-cat. Now, do we really want another? That's what we should be asking ourselves."

As Tycho and he joked, they looked at each other with deepening dismay and alarm. But suddenly Richard's face changed. His eyes grew sharp and accusing.

"What the hell have you been up to?" he cried. Tycho looked guiltily at his bed in case the shape of Angela was somehow pressed into it. "Your hands! They're bandaged,"

Richard said. He swung his feet off the bed and sat up slowly.

"Oh that!" Tycho said with relief. "That's nothing." He was saved from having to answer by Africa's voice out in the kitchen. She began speaking very loudly and with great passion.

"Dad, you don't understand. It's not *like* that. It's nothing Hudson's *done*. Look – I *loved* Hudson. I *dreamed* of Hudson. It used to be wonderful to do the dishes with bloody Hudson. And he hasn't changed. *I've* changed. I don't want to tidy up after Hudson, or cook delicious little meals for Hudson, or go to *bed* with Hudson."

"That's telling them," Tycho said, impressed. "Events are the stuff of the world and each of them is of brief duration."

"Don't you come the deep thinker over me," Richard cried. "What have you been up to? What have you done to yourself?"

"Oh no," said Africa, in the kitchen. "It's all very well calling it infatuation now. At the time it felt as real as anything could. Anyhow, who says it's got to last for ever to be real?"

Someone was walking up the drive. Tycho and Richard saw a head they did not recognise bob past their window.

"No, I'm sorry, Dad," Africa was saying. "I don't want to hurt your feelings," (Richard groaned softly) "but a lot of you people stayed together because you were too poor to do anything else. Don't try and build it into a great virtue."

"Who was that coming in?" Richard asked, still staring at Tycho's hands.

"Hudson's lawyer," Tycho suggested.

"You'll have to leave home," Richard said suddenly.

"Why me?" Tycho asked, turning to him indignantly.

"Because you'll probably get a scholarship – an A-bursary at the very least – if you're half as good as you make out," Richard said. "It doesn't matter which – it's only an extra dollar or two every week. It's an income. Add on to that our home circumstances, you'll get a hardship-allowance to live away from home. With Dad being the way he is, he's definitely lower-income group. You're a sitter for all the benefits you can get at university. You're the logical one."

"Have you ever heard of getting a job?" Tycho hissed at him. "It's spelt W-O-R-K and pronounced 'work'."

"Oh, yeah – I know!" Richard said. "I know I'll have to do something! I just don't want to spend my life doing something I hate. But let's face it, it's going to be rugged here. You heard them."

They both turned their heads as they heard, very faintly, a knock on the back door.

"Mum wants them back together again," Richard said. "At present she wants the marriage to last, even if the people involved don't. 'You can't expect to be ecstatically happy,' she keeps on saying. But why not? If we're given the power to be ecstatic why not aim for it?"

"Suppose she sometimes felt like leaving Dad…" Tycho began.

"I'm on Africa's side," Richard said. "It's over. There's no chemistry. The only way they can get a spark out of each other is by fighting. Love doesn't last. It's not meant to."

"But Mum and Dad have been married twenty-five years," Tycho said. Richard shook his head.

"Oh that!" he said helplessly. "You can't count that."

"I think you have to," Tycho said, but he didn't quite know how.

"I'll count it as loyalty, not love," Richard said. "Who *is* that out there?"

Mrs Potter's unmistakable footsteps came down the hall.

"Tycho!" she cried, almost accusingly. "What have you been up to? There's someone from the paper out there with a photographer in tow. Tycho, we don't want anyone like that here. I've taken the phone off the hook in case Granny Potter rings. She often does ring on a Saturday morning. I'm just too topsy-turvy to cope."

"Tell them to go away then," Tycho said wearily. "I don't care."

"What the hell," said Richard slowly, "have you been up to? What have you done with your hands? Who tied them up so neatly for you?"

("How about a packet of instant Fame?" asked an unidentifiable retailer in Tycho's market-place, white-aproned like an old-fashioned grocer. "It's a very popular line, sir. Makes you irresistible to the ladies!" "I'd love to, but my mother won't let me," Tycho muttered.)

His mother stared at his hands, distressed because he was hurt, ashamed because she hadn't noticed it sooner, and above all horrified at the possibility of another crisis in a household already stretched by more crises than it could reasonably bear.

"Tycho! Why didn't you *say*?" She sighed, and ran her fingers through her hair in a poetic gesture of confusion.

Tycho held up his white hands like the gloved paws of a minstrel. *Cheerfulness is the goal of life,* Democritus advised him from his wall.

"Don't worry, Mum," he said. "Look! 'The Camp Town ladies sing this song, doo dah! Doo dah!' " he sang, and did his own version of a soft-shoe shuffle right into the carelessly misplaced ironing.

"Who put my clean washing on the *floor*?" Mrs Potter actually stamped her foot, something Tycho and Richard had not seen happen for years.

Tycho jarred his arm against a chest of drawers and winced with the pain in his hands. Someone came running down the hall and burst into the room. It was Africa.

"Come on, Tyke," she said. "Your public's waiting."

"Africa, not now!" Mrs Potter said. "We're all upside down."

"Mum – he pulled a man out of a burning car. He saved some guy's *life*!" Africa boomed like a foghorn. Tycho could have sworn he saw all the quotations vibrate like sympathetic butterflies.

"Africa, dear – have some mercy on us," Mrs Potter begged. "We've got more than enough to cope with as it is."

Africa looked at Tycho and, just for a moment, he saw a disconcerting ghost, a family likeness to himself that unexpectedly marked them as brother and sister.

"Mum, they don't want to talk to me about my marriage, and they don't want to talk to you about an untidy kitchen. They want to talk to Tyke. Tyke! He'll cope. None of the rest of us has to."

"Sounds as if he's coped all right so far," Richard said. "Off you go, Tyke, and be a three-minute hero. Andy Warhol," he remarked mysteriously. "I've got my set of quotations, too."

"If Tyke misses out on being a three-minute hero because of me I'll never forgive myself," Africa said. "God alone knows he needs something apart from all this!" Her gesture took in the room, and the telescope under his bed, the ironing on the floor, and the quotations on the walls. "Get them to take your photo holding Hamish and then, when he's grown up, Hamish will say, 'That's a picture of me with brave Uncle Tycho.'"

"Pity about the hands, though. He'll never play the violin again," Richard added.

"I'll learn to play it with my feet," Tycho said.

"Oh, he's strong! Strong!" Richard cried, pushing him towards the door.

"It's the love of a good sister that saved him," Africa said, seizing his arm and hurrying him past his mother into the hall. "Love changes and wears out," she muttered to him, and she was the second woman he had seen shedding tears that morning, though over a different sort of love. "But if you do a brave thing it lasts as long as you do."

("It's guaranteed a lifetime," said the retailer in the market-place smugly. "Good value!" "It's just an impulse buy," Tycho muttered to himself, accepting the offer.)

16

THE CATALOGUE OF THE UNIVERSE

When the phone rang Angela leapt in from the verandah expecting it to be Tycho. She was astonished at her own excitement, seized the phone and hunched herself around it, preparing to shut herself in with his voice.

"Am I speaking to Angela May?" asked a woman whose crisp tones she certainly remembered from somewhere. At first Angela thought it might be the newspaper people again, though the voice did not have the democratic warmth she associated with the reporter who had rung to ask her about the car crash below Dry Creek bridge. She got the impression of a voice made tight by nervousness.

"That's right!" she said. "This is me."

"Angela, this is the other Angela – your grandmother," said the voice. "Did your mother tell you I rang you earlier."

"Yes, she did tell me," Angela said.

"Did she tell you I wanted to speak to you?" the voice asked, even more nervously.

"She did say something about it," Angela replied, her fingers tightening on the receiver. Mrs Chase's nervousness was making her nervous herself and this usually meant she also began to feel irritable. "Actually, I thought I wouldn't bother to ring back, because there seemed to be a lot of doubt about it – whether you were my grandmother at all, I mean." There was a hesitation at the other end of the phone. "Not that I really care now," Angela added quickly.

"Ro was very upset, you know," said Mrs Chase. "You came as such a shock to us. In spite of what you might think, he's a sensitive man. He was very upset over Dido. I have to take some of the responsibility for that, you know. I..."

"He can't have been all that upset," Angela said. "I found him easily enough when I wanted to. He could have found us."

"He lives under a lot of pressure these days," his mother went on, as if she hadn't heard Angela's comment. "I've talked it over with him, my dear, and – well, I'd like to meet you somewhere and talk in a more civilised way than was possible yesterday. He's so guilty about the past, poor boy, but between us we might be able to bring him round..."

"Not possible!" Angela cried. It alarmed her to be pursued by this elegant whippet and she wondered briefly if Roland Chase had felt anything like this on seeing her in the waiting-room outside his office. "Why now, anyhow? You've never wondered about us before."

"No," the other Angela admitted. "No, I haven't." (She gave a small, embarrassed laugh.) "I have to admit that seeing you made a lot of difference. You look so like Ro. I suppose I always wondered – but seeing you, there was no doubt in my mind that you were his little girl."

"I'm *not* his little girl," Angela cried angrily and almost put the phone down, but not quite. She was more curious than she wanted to be.

"I didn't know your mother very well," Mrs Chase began and then stopped. "Did she tell you that I came to visit her after – that is, before you were born?"

"She just told me this afternoon," Angela said, for she had talked many things over with Dido and knew Mrs Chase had not wanted her to be born. Mrs Chase had given Dido money for an abortion.

"My dear, try and understand," Mrs Chase said. "Ro's whole future was at stake..."

"Mine too!" said Angela, but she said it without any bitterness. She merely wanted the conversation to end. "Look, I'm sorry I came to see him. I made a mistake. I don't want to think about it any more," and she hung up quickly and rather rudely, for she found a despicably wistful memory of the blue swimming pool nudging her, and she did not want to find herself thinking of Roland Chase and his possessions ever again.

"Who was that?" Dido asked, as she came back on to the verandah once more.

"Guess who!" Angela said, pulling a face.

"Oh her," said Dido. "Good heavens! You might have missed out on a father, but you seem to have nailed a granny!"

"I don't want a granny," Angela said crossly. "She likes me because I look like her darling son. She's even taking part of the blame herself – for him, I mean!"

"She probably ought to," Dido said. "I'm sure they sent him away you know – his parents did, I mean. I told him you were on the way, he said we'd get married, I said a radiant goodnight to him and never saw him again. He was over in Australia on a long visit to some cousins before you could say Jack Robinson. Believe me, I had no idea his mother was called Angela. I didn't know anyone who knew the family. I didn't hear her name mentioned. When I asked Ro what names he liked he mentioned Angela for a girl and I simply accepted that." She shook her head. "I expect he simply picked the first name to come into his head. I treated it like gospel."

"It means 'messenger'," Angela reminded her. "What message did I bring?" She had asked this question before and loved the answer.

"You were the message," said Dido very dryly.

The brilliant day, in which time had been so concentrated that Angela had been born, loved, orphaned, had died and been reborn all during a single morning, was slowly fading into evening. Along the familiar line between trees, with their sequinned edging of city lights, and the sky, the clouds had curdled a little and the air was like very dark blue grass, coloured but so clear you could look deeply into it and find no ending. The brightest constellations were beginning to show, the planets were already bright, Jupiter in the upper west, Venus very low on the horizon. In the constellation of the compasses the red star Aldebaran shone, and Angela looked at it and thought about Amalthea, the reddest object in the solar system.

I'm longing for old Tyke, she thought. I've done it. I've fallen in love with him. I've always wanted to in a way, but now I've managed it. She was not sure how or even why. She had known all the good things about him for a long time, so it was not as if she had suddenly realised what they were. And his shadowy view of things did not match hers. Nevertheless, now she had been reunited and reconciled with Dido, all she could think of was seeing Tycho once more, and mixed in with this was a curious feeling of triumph, as if in the end she had won a victory and had forced the indifferent universe to render up a sort of justice.

The verandah had no lights, but lights were on in the living room behind them. Moths tapped softly on the glass. Occasionally the thin voice of a mosquito made itself heard, causing them to look suspiciously into the dusk. There was nothing worse to bother them. Angela had confessed her detective work, which had given her a clue to her father's whereabouts, and had told about her slow approaches to him over the last fortnight.

"I wrote that letter ages ago," Dido said reminiscently. "I wrote it when you were very small. I asked him to make sure you were looked after if anything happened to me. I suppose, if I'm honest, it was another way of keeping him in my life, because what I told you wasn't all lies. I just adored

Ro, though now I can't remember that he said or did anything remarkable, and I can't help wondering if it was mainly because he was so good-looking. I couldn't believe he'd chosen me," Dido said. "Just having him in my thoughts made every day seem marvellous." Dido slapped her own arm, thinking a mosquito had landed there. "It's a lovely evening, sitting out here, but would you mind if we moved in? There's still the dishes to do. People can say what they like about the eternal verities, love and truth and so on, but nothing's as eternal as the dishes."

"I like it that you took money from the old whippet and spent it on a pram and baby-clothes and things..."

"And a bottle of wine," Dido said. "I drank my own health."

"Some people would have been too proud to take the money," Angela went on. "I think that would have been silly."

"Truly, I was desperate," Dido confessed. "I didn't know what I was going to do, except that I was determined to keep you. I felt I knew you already. Mind you, I thought you were a boy, but apart from that..."

Dido had got work through the hospital with a doctor and his family doing ironing and housework ("They ironed their tea towels," she exclaimed in wonder) and had then scraped along, taking her baby with her, through a disjointed series of housekeeping jobs, none of which had been pleasant or settled, until she went to work for the old man, Tommy Forrester, who had liked her and had not minded that she was slow at housework. ("I didn't feel too

good for it," Dido said. "I felt not good enough. Dreadful!")
And during that time she had saved enough to rent 1000
Dry Creek Road, a cottage where nobody else wanted to live.
Later they had been able to buy it.

"And live happily ever after!" cried Angela triumphantly.

"More or less," said Dido. "We've got this far anyway."

They carried the dishes into their tiny kitchen. Along the
windowsill, things Dido had collected were set out in a line,
a little seahorse, dry as an autumn leaf, a helical shell curled
round and round on itself, a piece of glass washed up by the
sea. Bunches of papery flowers hung upside down, drying at
the window, and at one end of the counter sat a pottery owl
with hollow eyes, really intended as an incense-burner. The
little kitchen smelled of herbs and newly-baked bread, for
while Angela had slept that afternoon, Dido had baked two
loaves of bread. They sat there at the end of the counter
covered with a clean tea towel. There was no lightshade. The
naked bulb poured gold down on them and outside, the
window tapped and seethed with moths. Some of them were
no more than threads of brown silk, others large, equilateral
triangles, climbing up the glass, their prismatic eyes
occasionally catching the light and making it look as if their
heads were studded with jewels.

"It's a real adventure story," Angela said enthusiastically,
scraping scraps into the compost bucket.

"Well, I got by," Dido said, "but it was touch and go
sometimes. In the beginning, I felt sure I was strong enough,
and so I was as it turned out, but only *just*. And you said

something the other day which is true... that sometimes, in getting the better of things, I've put too much of myself into my disadvantages. That old letter you found, I've seen it there in my file for years and I've thought, why don't I throw this away? But I've kept it because it was a sign of where I'd been. Anyhow, on Monday I'll start searching for a builder who'll put a door between the bedrooms and the living room, if I can find one who'll drive up this hill and bring timber along the track. Failing that I'll get a joinery book and have a crack at it myself."

"What about the outside loo?" Angela asked.

"I think a septic tank might cost an arm and a leg," Dido said doubtfully. "I'll ask, though. Outside lavatory or not, I love this place."

"Me too," Angela said, remembering their first meal there, and the moths, probably ancestors of this evening's moths, tapping at this very window.

"You didn't have to tell me all that stuff about my father," Angela said. "I would have been happy without it."

"Well, everyone told me – the nurse at the hospital and the social worker and everyone – how important it was for a child to have two loving parents, and how bad it is for them to feel rejected," Dido said, rather humbly. "I wanted you to have everything I could give you and much more. And then I suppose I was telling myself the story as much as I told it to you. I mean, I wished it had been like that." She stirred the washing-up water with the dishmop, making another galactic spiral as she did so. "It was partly true any way. I *did* love Ro. It was just that he didn't love me."

"It must have been awful," Angela said, trying to acknowledge the past. But, after all, it was ages ago, and as Dido herself kept on saying, everything had changed since then.

"Sometimes I thought it would kill me," Dido said briefly. "But it didn't," she went on. "Anyhow, I suppose deep down I went on hoping for years that I'd go to the door and Ro would be there. The phone would go, or there'd be a knock I wasn't expecting and... but I've grown to love solitude more than almost anything."

"Making the best of a bad job," Angela suggested sceptically.

"Not quite," Dido said. "I've had a lot of practice at that, but I've chosen, too." She propped a plate against a cup. "That's it," she said, and pulled the plug out. The water made a wonderful spiral running out of the plug hole.

"There's this idea called the doctrine of signatures," Angela began vaguely, but she could only remember Tycho mentioning it, nothing that he had said about it. "I nearly died when I saw the car fall," she said solemnly. "I was getting a feeling of doom and then..."

"Not us *this* time," Dido said. "I had a feeling of doom too, but maybe it was just you and your questions. Maybe I knew I was going to be found out. It isn't often I lose my nerve, but I did when you got so interested. I froze up. Yet I don't usually have any trouble telling the truth. I just hoped your interest might fade away, like believing in Santa Claus."

"But the road *is* like a sign," Angela said. "Of travelling dangerously."

"Yes," Dido agreed. "I love living up here in the teeth of the wind, right under the sky, nothing between me and the hills. I read and cut the grass and make bread... it's part of me for ever, and it'll stay on even when you're gone."

Angela did not deny that she would go someday soon.

"You could write a book when I'm not here any more," she said.

"I'll finish my degree first," Dido said. "And then I might – oh, there's so many things... scythe grass for people with overgrown lawns. Or learn how to make clocks!"

Angela liked the thought of making clocks.

"I'll help you," she said. "Not those sickly chiming clocks though. We'll make clocks that laugh and mutter to themselves. We'll be Old Mother Time and her everlasting daughter." There was a slight intensification of light in the kitchen like a fluctuation of the power source. Angela and Dido both knew it was the headlights of a car finding a tiny gap in the trees.

"The dreaded granny," Dido said, smiling a little maliciously at Angela. "You *will* get yourself into these things."

"It'll be Tyke," Angela said. For the life of her she couldn't prevent her face lighting up. "Little old Tyke," she said, with a creditable imitation of yesterday's feeling. "I'll go and meet him."

Dido watched her sling her tea towel over the rail and said, straightening it up after her, "Oh yes? And since when do you go charging off into the dark to meet Tycho Potter? He's always managed to find his own way up the hill before now."

"You suspicious old woman!" Angela cried. "He's a bit of a hero now, isn't he? He's a little toughy in his way. Did you notice the front of his hair was frizzled by the fire. It was that close. Anyhow, you like him, don't you? He's very mysterious, in a sort of troubled way."

Then she went off into the warm, starry night, scorning to take a torch. Something brushed against her face, but Angela knew it was only the leaves of an elderberry tree. The scuttle on her left did not alarm her for she was in her own place, and she knew the scuttler for a simple summer hedgehog.

"Keep off the road," she advised it, but hedgehogs, like people, couldn't always be relied on to take good advice. Coming down the track, as confidently as if she could see every step and stone, she sang a song the school choir had been practising for the break-up. Tycho, getting out of his car below, heard the song, floating out of the night towards him, and his scorched hair crawled on his head.

"*A great while ago the world began,*" sang Angela.
"*With hey, ho, the wind and the rain.*
But that's all one, our play is done,
And we'll strive to please you everyday.
Tyke!" she said, stepping out of the shadows.

"Hi!" said Tycho cautiously, the hair still tingling on his scalp, for the air had spoken to him in a magical voice, Angela's voice, and the voice of a lot of other things besides.

"Very cool, Big Science!" Angela said admiringly. "Have you lost interest in me already?"

"Shut up!" Tycho said. "It's just I can't believe today. Nothing's happened for years, and then suddenly everything has."

"Sit down here for a moment," Angela said, and they sat on the bottom step, almost invisible to one another, for there was no light to see by except starlight and a faint glow from the house, seeping down through the leaves.

"How's things anyway?" Tycho asked.

"Fine!" Angela said. "Everything's fine. I'll count them off. Item one, Dido and I have forgiven each other and I'm going to be a wonderful daughter for ever after. Item two, she told me that false love story because she wanted me to think I had a caring father somewhere out there. Item three, I'm having a little go at being in love with you, so why has your phone been engaged all day? Are you playing hard to get?"

"The phone's off the hook because Africa's moved back home," Tycho explained, rather gloomily. "She's fallen in love with a lecturer at her university extension course which is meant to stop women at home from becoming cabbages."

"Gosh, it's worked, hasn't it?" Angela said. "It wasn't just theory. But why does the phone have to be off the hook?"

"Mum's not too pleased at the papers calling to get my

impressions of the car crash," Tycho explained. "And we're frightened Granny Potter might ring. Or Hudson."

"She should be thrilled!" Angela cried indignantly. "You were brave."

Tycho did not try to deny this. He felt more and more that it must be true. "She's not against me saving someone's life," he said, "but she thinks I chose the wrong time to do it. Not quite that – it's just that she's upset over Africa and doesn't like it being mixed up with other things."

"But wasn't Africa completely crazy over Hudson?" Angela asked.

"That was last year," Tycho said.

Angela could remember the rich dramas of Africa's wedding, and now another teasing memory began to work itself in and out of these recollections.

"Hang on a moment!" she said. "What were you telling me the other day about Pythagoras?"

"In any right-angled triangle," Tycho began doubtfully, "the square on the hypotenuse..."

"Not that!" Angela said scornfully. "No, I remember now. He tried to keep it a secret. The square root of two was an irrational number. Well, it still is, isn't it, and people are still trying to pretend differently."

"That's really coarse," Tycho said, after considering this.

"You're just jealous because you didn't think of it," Angela said. "I didn't invent it. The Ionians did."

"The Pythagoreans!" Tycho said. "A different lot! Mystics not scientists."

"Some ancient Greeks, anyway," Angela said. "All the same, even if it is irrational, you've got to have a go, haven't you? You've got to believe that you're the one who's going to get it right, or where's the sense of it? I didn't tell Dido anything about last night. I just made out we'd sat around talking and drinking coffee, like real intellectuals." In the dark, Tycho looked extremely grateful. "I want to have you for myself for a bit," Angela said thoughtfully.

"Me too!" Tycho said. "What with Africa being home, life's a bit too rich at our place at present."

Angela leaned against him.

"What with knowing you so well, I feel as if we've been married for ages in a way," she said, "probably during that eclipse – do you remember – ages ago?"

Tycho certainly remembered.

"The moon's shadow went over us both and married us. Nothing can be done about it. You can't get a divorce, not after the moon's shadow. That's a good romantic notion."

They kissed each other with the romantic notion still lively in their thoughts.

"Why are you wearing gloves?" Angela asked, and then cried, "It's bandages, isn't it? Are you all right?"

"I'm better now," Tycho said, but Angela made him stand up and followed him up the track.

"We'd better get in or Dido will be suspicious," she told him firmly.

Tycho obeyed, only to be very disconcerted by Dido's first glance which seemed very complex indeed. However, all she said was, "Well, what a hero *you've* turned out to be!"

"I'll have to wait and see," Tycho said. "I rang Phil Cherry and he says Jerry's in a very serious condition. They've taken his bad leg off, close to the knee. How do you think a guy like that will cope with crutches or a tin leg or whatever?"

Angela thought of Jerry and shivered.

"A dark angel flew by," Dido said, touching her shoulder. "They do, sometimes."

"Dark, but with burning wings," Angela agreed. "It didn't notice us. But poor Jerry!"

A curious thought struck her – even if he lived she would never get him mixed up with Phil again, and for some reason it made her sad, but she was too pleased to see Tycho to be sad for long.

"It's ruined your hair so now you'll have to put yourself in my hands. Dido, I'm going to improve old Tyke out of all recognition!" And saying this Angela hugged her mother, but looked sideways at Tycho who felt, at second hand, her arms around his neck and her skin against his. "I'll even forgive the old whippet, shall I? Shall I ring her and get her to take me out to some marvellous place and buy me pancakes, and strawberries and cream? I ought to do good for others." She saw Tycho looking at her disapprovingly. "It's not for *him*," she said quickly. "It really isn't. Because I look like him, it seems we belong together whether we want to or not, but I'm going to take this face over and make it all mine, and then, when he's old, people will say to him, 'Do you know who you remind me of? Wonderful Angela May. Now she really *is* the message.'"

Dido laughed and shook her head.

"I feel really sorry for the whippet," Angela went on. "For one thing she's got legs like little thin sticks and you can tell they've been like that all her life."

"Don't get too turned on by the prospect of doing good for others," Dido remarked, her laugh dying into a smile that interested Tycho, for it seemed a smile that might accompany secret, ironic thoughts. "I don't mind you being kind-hearted in principle, but be careful."

"It could count as a sort of revenge," Angela said.

"Living well is the best revenge," Dido said, quoting an old proverb.

Angela had said that she wanted to keep her changed relationship with Tycho a secret, but some other contrary wish made her also want to display it and she managed this by conducting a flirtation with the rest of the room, by the way she touched the table top, looked towards the window when the moths tapped loudly, or touched his shoulder as she walked past his chair.

"Your mother will guess a hundred times over," said Tycho in a low voice when Dido went out of the room.

"I'm not as used to having secrets as you," Angela said, a little penitently. "I want it secret and I want to tell, too. Anyhow, you seem a bit independent tonight. You can be as brave and famous as you like, but don't think it's all just a walk-over from now on."

"I know that," Tycho said. "I've worked that out, don't you worry."

"Well," Angela said, relenting, "you know what you're standing on. It might look as if it's up there over your head, but it's really under your feet, holding you up."

Tycho laughed. As he did so, Dido came back out of her minute kitchen, peeling an orange, looking at them like someone marvelling at a familiar but still disconcerting phenomenon, a look entertained, resigned, and even a little sad.

"I'll have to go," Tycho said, "or my mother will think I'm out looking for another burning car. It's been a full day – what with one thing and another." Then he added, looking rather defiantly at Dido, "I'm sorry I forgot to ring. It was just..."

"I know!" said Dido. "The black coffee was so good."

"I'll walk you down the track," Angela suggested, "in case you fall over in the dark."

But Tycho rarely stumbled in the dark. As he stood up, it seemed to him that everything that had happened in the last two days streamed into him, or out of him... he couldn't be sure which. There was light and dark, sun and stars, the air roared with traffic, rustled with hedgehogs, Hamish stood up, Mrs Chase reached out, Angela embraced him, and the car leapt and fell and burned. Half-transfixed, wearing what Angela thought of as his magician's look, Tycho felt himself actually become the catalogue of the universe, never finished, always being added to.

"Be very careful on the hill, won't you?" Dido said to him.

"Tyke? He drives so carefully it's like being in a funeral procession," Angela retorted.

"I was thinking of the bit before he even gets to the car," Dido said.

"Oh, ha ha! Very funny!" Angela said, perhaps giving up all idea of concealment. "It's as dangerous for me as it is for him, but you're not warning me. What sort of mother are you?"

"Are you not daughter enough to know?" Dido said. "Go on! Don't take for ever, but do take care. After all, it's been a long day."